A Horse to Remember

BY THE SAME AUTHOR

Draw Horses with Sam Savitt

The Viking Press, New York

A Horse to Remember

A NOVEL & ILLUSTRATIONS BY

SAM SAVITT

First Edition
First published in 1984 by The Viking Press
40 West 23rd Street, New York, New York 10010
Published simultaneously in Canada by Penguin Books Canada Limited

A Horse to Remember is an expanded and substantially changed version of
There Was a Horse, by Sam Savitt. Copyright © 1961 by Sam Savitt.
Printed in U.S.A.
1 2 3 4 5 88 87 86 85 84

Special acknowledgment to my friend Gordon Wright, master horseman and
unforgettable teacher.

Many thanks to Mike Smithwick, who won the Maryland Hunt Cup six
times.

Library of Congress Cataloging in Publication Data
Savitt, Sam.   A horse to remember.
Summary: When he learns that his newly acquired, uncontrollable
horse was formerly a racehorse of distinction, seventeen-year-old
Mike Benson and his horse train to race again.
[1. Horses—Fiction. 2. Horse racing—Fiction] I. Title.
PZ7.S266Ho 1984   [Fic]   83-16655   ISBN 0-670-37920-4

To Bette with love

A Horse to Remember

CHAPTER I

MY EYE KEPT COMING BACK TO THE BIG GRAY. HE WAS standing quietly inside the paddock with a motley assortment of browns and bays. I was standing on the outside, half listening to Big John go on about weather and politics, but my eye kept drifting back to the gray. Maybe it was just his color that caught my attention at first, although now I'd like to think it was something else—something much more important.

During my Easter vacation I had consulted eight horse dealers and chased down countless private leads. Crossing and crisscrossing my trail, I had driven about a thousand miles and had seen almost that many horses—all kinds, all shapes, sizes, breeds. It was the same story over and over again. The ones I liked I couldn't afford, and the ones I could afford I wouldn't have given stall room.

I had been at Big John's livery stable all afternoon. I had seen every horse on the place, including the cannery stuff standing in the paddock. Now it was time to go home.

"Be seeing you," I said, and turned to the pickup parked in the muddy driveway. I slid behind the wheel, the motor caught, and as the truck moved forward, I glanced back for one more look at the gray. The last rays of the late March sun slanted across the barnyard, spotlighting the horses bunched together in the paddock. Suddenly the gray's head came up, turning toward my truck. There was a bold, defiant look about him, and for one brief instant the sight of the gray horse against the red barn in the brilliant sunlight dazzled my eye.

I pushed my foot down hard on the brake. My mind was made up. I climbed out and slogged back through the mud to where John was still standing.

I planted myself in front of him and asked as coolly as I could, "How much do you want for that gray horse?"

"He's worth a thousand," John answered slowly.

"I've got four hundred and sixty-two dollars," I parried, as I brought out of my coat pocket a tight roll of bills held together by a thick rubber band.

John scratched his black beard and rested his huge bulk against a paddock post.

I thrust the roll of bills in the direction of the gray horse.

"Look at him," I went on. "He's nothing but skin and bones. The meat packers won't give you this much for him."

The last statement made up John's mind. He couldn't deny the fact that the gray horse wasn't worth much on the hoof, and as far as the horse's potential as a show or hunter prospect was concerned, that had to be a long way down the road.

"He's all yours," John grunted as he reached for my money.

That's the way it all began. Next morning I picked up the gray in my one-horse trailer, and all the way home I kept asking myself what it was about this horse I liked so much. He certainly wasn't much to look at. True, his color was attractive, but no sane horseman will buy a horse for that reason. He stood about 16.3. His rugged, rawboned frame pressed sharply outward, trying to poke through the taut dappled-gray hide. The legs were straight, though, and hard—no serious-looking bumps—but his barrel was a bit long, with a high, prominent wither that would cut a man in two if he was stupid enough to ride him bareback. A long, skinny neck joined a good sloping shoulder and neat thoroughbred head. The ears were small, curvy; the eyes were warm, dark, set in a broad forehead that bulged slightly, then dished downward to the flaring nostrils of his Arabian ancestry. The whole picture of him was roughly drawn, like the start of a painting with the sketch lines in and the finish a long way off. I'd seen better-looking horses, but I had also seen worse.

I'm supposed to be a pretty fair horseman, and I know better than to buy a horse just because I like the look in his eye. But, so help me, I think that's the only reason I bought this bag of bones. He had a look. I'm sure it was all in my imagination, but there was something in his eye—like a warm memory of time gone by, or maybe a bright flash into the future. I sensed a challenge—and a promise. I couldn't resist them.

It was almost four in the afternoon when I pulled into our barnyard. My brother, Chris, came up from the barn to meet me. He was only ten years older than I, but Chris had been mother and father to me ever since our parents died in an auto accident almost six years ago.

Nettie, our housekeeper, also came down from the house to watch the unveiling. She had worked for Mom and Dad as far back as I could remember, and after they were gone, she moved in and took over. She ran a tight ship; even though her eyesight was poor and she wasn't as spry as she used to be, Nettie managed to keep track of everything that went on, in the house and out of it.

Chris helped me unhitch and drop the tailgate, then he leaned his spare frame against the fence and lit his pipe. My gray charger backed down the ramp as if he were a hundred, and when he finally jolted to a halt in the yard and planted himself with half-shut eyes and drooping lower lip, he looked even worse.

"This the horse that's going to help buy us a new tractor?" I couldn't tell whether Chris was asking me or telling me, but I nodded and looked him straight in the eye.

"Okay," he muttered. "Put him away for now and let's get on with the milking."

Nettie made no comment as she turned and hurried back up to the house.

I knew Chris didn't think much of my new horse, and I could hardly blame him. I was beginning to have doubts, too.

The following morning Doc Steiner, our local vet, came by. He was also a long-time friend of the family.

"How you doing, Mike?" he greeted me as he stepped out of his truck. "So you've got yourself a new horse."

I'm afraid he's not very new, I thought to myself. I really liked Doc Steiner. He was not only a nice guy but a top veterinarian. Often during school vacations I would accompany him on his rounds. It was a real treat, for I loved caring for animals, especially sick ones.

"It's a daily challenge," Doc would say. "Sick people let you know how they feel—where they hurt. But with animals you've got to find out all by yourself 'cause they don't talk. You'd make a good vet, Mike," he would tell me for the hundredth time. "You've got a natural feel for it, an instinct that doesn't come out of a book. Think about it."

Now that I was seventeen and almost out of high school, I thought about it a lot, particularly at this moment as I admired the positive and knowledgeable way his hands probed every part of the gray horse.

Finally he turned to me and grinned. There was a twinkle in his eye as he asked, "How old would you say this horse is, Mike?"

"About nine or ten, no more," I answered positively, then quickly added, "The brownish-colored groove on the corner incisor teeth has just appeared. This is called the Galvayn's mark, which gradually runs down the tooth and finally disappears at about the age of twenty—that right, teacher?"

"Right on target, Mike." The doc chuckled. "As I said before, you'd make a fine vet."

Doc Steiner walked back to his truck and returned with a syringe. He inserted the nozzle of it into the corner of the gray's mouth. One quick squirt and he was finished.

"This will take care of the worms for now," he predicted. "I'll follow up with a worming program every three months. Otherwise, he's not in as bad shape as he looks."

When the doc had driven off and I was leading the gray horse back to his stall, I noticed for the first time a thin jagged scar, barely discernible through the dapples, halfway down his left shoulder. I ran my fingers over it. This horse has been around, I thought, but I knew I'd learn more about him sitting on his back. Right now all he needed was lots of rest and feed and love.

At first he was pretty listless. He would stand for hours at a time, barely touching his food, scarcely glancing in my direction when I walked into his stall. I hand-fed him, coaxing, stroking his thin neck, but it was a long time before I again saw the spark in his eye that first caught my attention at Big John's stable.

Late one afternoon my girl friend, Jennifer, came over to see how he was doing. I had told her about my horse right after I'd gotten him, but this was the first time she had come over to see him. Nettie brought out some fresh doughnuts she had just made.

"You should come more often," she admonished Jenny. "It's nice to see a pretty young girl in the house for a change."

She gave me a sharp poke in the ribs before she hustled back to the kitchen. Afterward Jenny and I walked down to the barn. As we stepped inside, a soft nicker greeted us.

"It must be you, Jenny!" I exclaimed. "This is the first positive sound this horse has made since he got here. He's on his way now!"

The gray's head came over the stall door as we approached. His expression was at once alert and inviting. Jenny hung back for a moment.

"Go ahead, Jen," I urged her. "He won't hurt you. He wants to be friendly."

Jenny cautiously touched his velvet muzzle, then let her fingers drift upward, scratching him gently on the cheek and forehead. I was beaming like a proud parent.

"He has such nice eyes," she said dreamily. "They're so soft and brown."

Jenny had always been lukewarm about horses, but seeing her like this—holding the gray's head cradled in her arms—made me feel great.

After I fed the gray horse, we sat together on the feed bin, listening to him munch his grain. What a pleasant, peaceful sound. I glanced over at Jenny. Her eyes were closed, and there was a whisper of a smile on her mouth. I leaned over and kissed her gently on the lips.

As the weeks rolled by, good feed started to take effect. Early in April the new spring grass began pushing up, the first haze of green deepened in the fields, and it did my heart good to watch the gray horse moving slowly across the pasture with his nose buried in its glittering richness. His coat took on a new luster. The hidebound look disappeared as his flanks filled and his belly dropped. Not once during all that time did I put a bit in his mouth or a saddle on his back.

When I wasn't working with Chris, I was admiring my horse. When I wasn't doing either, I was trying to maintain an A average in my senior year at Purdy High.

After Jenny's visit I began seeing her more often. Sometimes we did our homework together. I had to admit she was a lot smarter than I was, and I found out that the only thing I knew more about was horses. I got a chance to show off my knowledge when I took her to the Ox Ridge horse show in Connecticut.

"Oh, he's pulling on that horse's mouth. Why doesn't the rider let him go?" she exclaimed once, as we watched a jumper rider guide a big moving bay horse over a course of some scary-looking obstacles.

"He's not pulling on his horse's mouth," I explained patiently. "He's controlling his horse's pace so that he can meet his fences in stride and be right for takeoff."

By the end of the show Jennifer knew a lot more about horses than when she came in. And I found I got a kick out of pointing out to her what to look for and how the different classes were judged.

However, Jenny had never quite forgiven me for spending my entire Easter vacation horse-shopping. "Michael Benson," she said, "don't you know there are other things in life besides horses? Isn't it high time you began thinking about the future and what you're going to be?"

She was right—but I didn't like being nagged about it. I'd loved horses since I was little, and no girl was going to change that, even if she was my steady and pretty as a thoroughbred filly. I was completely relaxed and comfortable around horses, but girls always put me on the defensive, like the afternoon Jenny turned her big blue eyes on me when we were on the school bus.

"What are you thinking about, Mike?"

If I told her I was thinking about my horse, she'd be annoyed, so I said, "I was thinking about you."

"What about me?"

"Oh—I was thinking how pretty you are—and how nicely that sweater goes with your brown hair."

There I was, getting backed into a corner again and saying things I didn't want to say. The bus stopped at our driveway in the nick of time, and I mumbled a quick "So long," and lunged for the doorway. I hit the ground running, and only then did I realize how hot and stuffy that bus had become and how close I had come to saying too much.

Between school and Jenny and the farm, I hadn't gotten around to naming the gray horse, but I had taught him to come when I whistled. Sitting on the pasture fence just before feeding time, I let go with a long, shrill blast. His head came up, eyes and nostrils bringing me into quick focus. I whistled again, holding his attention, but after a moment he went back to the serious business of eating. A horse is a timid animal, always ready for flight, but also full of curiosity. Eventually, after three or four days, he had to investigate the whistle. I rewarded him with a carrot or a lump of sugar and a good scratch between the ears, and before long my bird call seldom failed.

Repetition and association are the keys to training a horse. He has a simple, one-track mind with a terrific memory. I remember a pony named Peaches I had when I was a kid. We were riding down Old Ridgebury Road once when a cat jumped out of a culvert right under Peaches' nose, and she nearly jumped out of her skin.

You know, I rode that pony for another seven years, and every time we passed that culvert she spooked like a three-year-old filly.

Up to this point the gray horse followed the book. He had good stable manners—gentle, affectionate—and we got along fine. Of course, handling a horse on the ground and riding him are completely separate relationships. But we'd cross that bridge when we came to it.

CHAPTER II

JUNE ARRIVED AND PASSED SWIFTLY WITH THE LAST OF my high school days. The senior outing was held at Paradise Lake in Bear Mountain State Park. The day was beautiful, sunny and warm. Of course, Jenny was my date. We all headed for the water as soon as we arrived, and it wasn't too long before the swimming became competitive. I had beaten all the guys, and Jenny had easily defeated the girls.

"How about a match race between Jenny and Mike?" my friend Marty Cole suggested.

Now I'm a pretty fair swimmer, but I was no match for Jenny. She could beat me hands down. I knew it, and she knew it. I was willing to try, but Jenny would have no part of it. "Aw, come on, Jenny," Marty teased. "Don't be chicken."

Wendy, his date, cut him down. "Lay off, Marty. You're becoming a bore." With that she turned away and faced the kids standing around. "How about our school song?" she asked, and soon the woods rang out with the long, sad notes of our alma mater.

Jenny was standing beside me. I reached over and took her hand and felt her fingers curl around mine. My voice rang out louder than usual. Marty was dead wrong, for there was nothing chicken about Jenny. She never afterward mentioned the incident, but I knew Jenny would not race me because she didn't want me to lose.

Graduation night was warm and soft, with the heady smells of early summer and fresh-cut hay. The publisher of the local newspaper was our principal speaker, but what he had to say about our future goals sounded like Jenny talking. I received my diploma along with thirty classmates. Our six-piece school band played "Finlandia," and we marched off the stage with heads high, clutching our rolled-up parchment passports to the future.

I had my brother's car and a date with Jenny following the graduation exercises.

After a bone-crushing handshake from Chris and affectionate bear hugs from Nettie and Jennifer's mother, we headed down the front steps and ran smack into Marty Cole coming from the opposite way.

"What's up, Marty?" I asked him. "You look lost. Where's Wendy?"

"She stood me up, Mike." There were tears in his eyes. "I wanted us to be alone, but she preferred to go dancing with the others—" His voice broke.

I placed a comforting hand on his shoulder. "That's a woman for you," I said consolingly. "She's gotta have it her own way."

"She's gotta have it her own way!" Jenny's voice nearly knocked me over. "You should talk, Mike. That's typical of you. There are only two ways to go—the wrong way and Mike's way!" Jenny's eyes were on fire, and she was angry. I was stopped in my tracks, speechless. Her burst of temper flared, then vanished as quickly as it came. She turned to Marty. "Why don't you come along with us? I'm sorry it turned out this way."

No sorrier than I was. In dead silence we drove down to Peach Lake. I parked near the pavilion. There was the sound of a rock band coming from inside. We got out and walked along the lakefront, away from the music. Marty was on the verge of crying, and Jenny was clucking over him like a mother hen, and every time I opened my mouth she told me to keep quiet.

Later I dropped Marty at his door. When I was driving Jenny home, I finally broke the silence.

"Jen, am I really like that, always having my own way?"

Jenny answered quietly; there was no sharpness in her voice now. "I'm afraid you are, Mike. I've never said anything about it—I hoped maybe you'd get over it."

I stopped the car in front of her house. "Honest, Jen, I didn't think I was like that. You know I'd never do anything to hurt you. I always thought I was considerate of the way you felt about things. Tell me when I wasn't."

Jenny's response came hesitantly. "Remember the time I wanted to go to the concert at Brewster Hall and you wanted to go to the horse show in Stamford? Well, we went to Stamford. And the art exhibit in Somers. You had a date with a horse somewhere, so I went along with you to watch." She thought for a moment. "How about the party at Wendy's? I wanted to be there, but you dragged me off to a movie you were anxious to see in Bedford. I can come up with more if you want me to."

I held up my hand. "No, thanks, you said enough." But I went on from there in my own mind, and I began to recall other times when I'd been guilty of just the sort of things Jenny had mentioned. I was surprised by it all— and disturbed.

"Mike, you're so quiet." Jenny's voice broke into my thoughts.

I couldn't bring myself to ask her forgiveness, but I did manage, "I'm sorry, Jen. I'll try to be different from now on."

Jenny kissed me on the cheek, and with a quick, "See you," she was out of the car. At her door she turned and waved good night. I drove slowly home.

I left the car in the garage and sat on the pasture barway, listening to the crickets and watching my gray horse graze in the moonlight. Girls are so complicated, so hard to understand.

Chris knew I loved horses, but Chris was a man who firmly believed that every animal and every person on the place should earn his keep, and I was to be no exception. "I don't mind your keeping the horse, Mike," he announced to me one evening at dinner. "But while you're trying to decide what you're going to do with the rest of your life, I expect you to carry your share of the work around here."

I had a lot of respect for Chris. I felt he was more my father than my brother. After all, he'd been looking after me since I was about eleven years old. He was a bit taller than I, but bone-hard, with rounded shoulders—probably from carrying the farm on his back. But Chris had loved the farm from the time he was a child riding a tractor beside Dad. It was a part of his life he never grew away from. And as time went on, he became more and more dedicated to it.

He'd been engaged to be married a few years back, but his bride-to-be decided she could not accept the life of a farmer's wife. And Chris was a farmer in every sense of the word. He wasn't much for small talk, but his voice was soft, and his eyes held a mixture of wisdom and humor, all of which combined to make any situation "no problem."

We had eighty-five cows—Holsteins and Swiss Charolais. Fifty were milked; the rest consisted of heifers and young stock. The horse barn was a hundred feet below the house; it was used mostly for hay storage now. But the cow barn, silo, and outbuildings were set way back, with more than two hundred acres of meadow and woods reaching out behind.

Jacob, an elderly ex-farmer from down the road, helped Chris with the daily chores, and during the school year I gave a hand whenever I had the time. But now I pitched in for real.

Chris and I rolled out of bed at 4:30 a.m. Dawn was just ahead as we hurried down to the barn. The milking apparatus was attached to the cows, and soon the barn came alive with the pulsating rhythm of the milking machines. The milk flowed through the overhead stainless-steel pipes and poured into the milk tank in an adjoining room.

"Remember, Mike," Chris reminded me, "the temperature in the tank must stay between thirty-four and thirty-eight degrees. If it gets any higher, bacteria quickly develop. So keep an eagle eye on the temperature gauge at all times."

The cows were being fed at the same time, and when the milking was over, we trudged back to the house. Nettie was up and about—the kitchen was filled with the delicious smells of breakfast. We ate in silence, then went back to the barn to turn out the cows.

In the cow barn a long, narrow concrete trench ran behind the place where the cows were fed and milked. After they were turned out for the day, the conveyor was turned on. All the manure was carried out of the barn and up a ramp onto the manure spreader. One of my jobs was to hook the tractor to it and spread the manure over one of the fields that was not being grazed at the time. Sometimes, working against a strong wind, I'd come back to the house so covered with manure that Nettie would make me undress in the mudroom and change my clothes before she would allow me inside.

The milk truck picked up our milk every morning at about eleven. As the milk gushed into the tank truck, I never failed to feel a wonderful surge of well-being, as if I were contributing to something important.

The cows were brought in at about four o'clock in the afternoon, and we went through the whole procedure again—feed, milk, clean up.

But this wasn't all there was to do. It was June, and we were right in the middle of the haying season. We grew our own but also had permission to cut other fields in the vicinity. The haying weather was great that summer—sunny, dry, and hot. If it should rain heavily between the time we cut and the time we baled—two days apart—the hay would be spoiled. So we worked frantically from sunup to sundown, keeping one eye on the heavens and praying for the good weather to continue.

By nightfall I was truly exhausted. I hardly looked in on the gray horse, just made sure he had plenty of food and water and was turned out daily. I talked to Jenny several times over the phone, but I was usually too tired to date.

Many evenings after supper and before bedtime I would sit on the top rail of the pasture fence and admire my horse. When I watched him gallop across a meadow, moving like silk, or halt on a rise of land, snorting and arching his neck into the wind, I was filled with pride. The challenge was still there.

CHAPTER III

ABOUT THE MIDDLE OF AUGUST I DECIDED IT WAS TIME to get the show on the road. Four new shoes, a grooming, and my gray horse was ready for action. He took the snaffle bit readily enough, but his back humped a little when I slid the saddle into place. I tightened the girth just enough to keep it from slipping and looped the bridle rein under the stirrup leathers. A halter went over the bridle, and one end of a lunge line was snapped to the halter ring. The rest of the line lay coiled in my left hand. He'd be pretty keen after his six months' layoff,

· 23 ·

and I intended to get the bucks out of him—take his edge off—before I got on.

Chris came along to watch. Our morning chores were finished—the cows had been turned out and the cow barn cleaned. I led my horse across the lower meadow through a barway and into a small natural ring, a level half-acre field completely surrounded by trees and stone walls. The gray was on his toes now, moving lightly with a quick, bouncing step. In the center of the ring I stopped and let him go on alone. When twenty feet of lunge line separated us, I clucked him into action. I was the hubcap, and he was the wheel. As he moved more strongly, I played out the line like a fisherman, always keeping a feel of his head and never letting him get behind me.

He went at it as if he'd done it before. He had good forward motion, so there were no problems. As he warmed up, his blood rose, exploding in a series of spine-twisting bucks that made me glad to be on the ground. He did nothing I didn't expect, and after ten minutes I brought him to a halt. The halter came off; I gathered the reins and swung aboard. He stood like a rock. I reached down, pulled up the girth a few holes, and we were ready to go to work.

It was the first time I had seen him from this position. The feel of him against my leg was just right, and his response was sharp and eager—almost too eager. I knew nothing about this horse. If he had started as a three-year-old, he had five years of experience behind him. He might have been a hunter, an open jumper, or even a racer—but I aimed to find out. You can learn a lot about a horse just by working around him, but the real message comes when you're sitting on his back riding him.

We worked slowly for almost an hour—walk, trot, canter, stop, back. He favored his left lead over the right, and he wasn't as soft in my hand as I would have liked him to be, but that would all come with time and with training.

During this exhibition Chris sat on the barway smoking his pipe. He made no comment, but I could see he was pleased. I was, too. It was too early to make predictions, but it looked as if I had myself a horse.

Our farm lay in a long valley in the heart of the Westchester hunt country. The land was rugged in spots, but most of it rolled gently through farm and woodland, crisscrossed by rushing streams and stone walls and post-and-rail fences.

The gray was doing well in the ring, but I was anxious to see what he could do on the outside. Some horses work well in an enclosure but will blow sky-high when they get in the open. This I had to find out. So far, he was too good to be true—so good, as a matter of fact, that my mind was filled with doubts and questions still unanswered. Why had a horse like this been on his way to the glue factory? What was his Achilles' heel? Where was the hole in him?

He passed the cross-county phase with flying colors.

He jumped well, coming into a fence a little too strongly, but standing off with a smooth, powerful thrust. Most horses will jump a stone wall better than a post-and-rail fence because the wall affords a good ground line that enables them to judge height and takeoff distance better. The gray horse was the opposite, preferring the rail fence. This in itself could mean nothing, but, on the other hand, it might be the first clue to his past, the first indication of what he had done before I found him.

Sometimes Jenny came along when I exercised my horse. She wasn't too good a rider, but she managed to hold her own on a well-schooled horse named Duke, borrowed from a neighbor across the road.

"This guy will take good care of you," I told her as I saddled him. "He's a nice quiet horse about the same age as the gray, nine or ten."

"Is nine or ten old?" Jenny asked.

"Gosh, no," I answered. "A horse doesn't really mature until he's five. And from nine to twelve he's in his prime, and if you treat him well he'll be working at twenty. In fact, that great racehorse Man o' War lived till the age of thirty-two."

She laughed nervously when she mounted for the first time. "Horses seem to sense my fear," she confided. "They act up. They know I'm afraid."

I disagreed. "Jenny, horses know nothing of the sort. You're the one who makes them act up."

I mounted the gray horse. "Here, let me show you what I mean," I explained. "When you're fearful, you get tight.

Your legs tighten and squeeze the horse. This is his signal to go." I pressed my legs to the gray's sides, and he instantly moved forward.

"But if I'm really fearful," I continued, "I pull back on the reins because I don't actually want him to go forward so quickly. In other words, I'm then telling my horse to go and stop at the same time—I'm clashing controls."

My horse became agitated, bouncing and tossing his head nervously as I demonstrated. When the gray settled down, we rode on. "You must never take any situation for granted," I warned. "There is no such thing as a foolproof horse, so always try to sense trouble before it happens."

Jenny's horse kept falling behind. Finally I pulled up to get her a switch. I legged my horse up under a tree, reached up and snapped off a thin branch for her to use as a crop. The loud snap of the breaking branch spooked the gray right out from under me. I hung in the air for one brief instant, then came to earth like a bale of hay coming down a hay chute. I sat there stunned for a moment, still clutching the broken branch.

Jenny retrieved the gray horse and brought him back to me. "Never take any situation for granted," she mimicked. "Remember, Michael, there is no such thing as a foolproof horse."

Up to this time the gray horse had filled all my expectations. A good type, well schooled, with manners and a nice way of going can bring a mighty fancy price in the hunt field. I had not made a pet of him. When you've lived on a farm all your life, buying and selling livestock is part of your daily existence, and you never let yourself get too deeply attached to an animal.

The Goldens Bridge Hounds was about to embark on another season of fox hunting. The official opening takes place on the first Saturday in October. But before then comes the cubbing in August, when the young hounds come out for the first time with the older ones to begin learning the sport. It is also a perfect time to test a green horse in the field under hunting conditions. The gray horse was ready to make his debut, and if the price was right, no matter how I felt about him, he would go.

Our family had been long-standing members of the hunt. Both my parents had hunted, and even Chris went out once in a while.

I had been out many times, mostly on green horses which had to be taught the finer points of fox hunting. There is an old saying that a good horseman is always mounted on a quiet horse. I considered myself a pretty fair horseman and planned to show off my horse exactly that way—steady, controlled, and, above all, quiet.

Hounds were meeting at the kennels that morning. I was up before dawn. The horse was fed and groomed. Our neighbor, Bill Uhlar, came over to help Chris while I was away. I rode out of the barnyard in the dark. There was a gentle coolness in the air, and as I hacked down the road, the east glowed pink with the sunrise. I had no premonition of what lay ahead, only the deep satisfaction that I was well-mounted and ready for anything. A big turnout was expected. Mark Shannon, a wealthy fox hunter from New York City, would be there, and rumor had it he was looking for a new horse. Let me see—what would I ask? Thirty-five hundred seemed about right—or maybe four thousand. My mind was spinning a web of dollar bills.

At Baxter Corner I ran into several friends on horseback, and we jogged along together. Shortly before I reached the meeting point, Wheeler, Mr. Shannon's man, rode up alongside. "Hey, Mike, that's quite a horse you've got there!" Play it cool, I thought—this is only the first nibble.

On this happy note I rode into the assembly area. The moment I arrived I felt something was wrong. I couldn't put my finger on it at first, then suddenly I became aware of a strange trembling sensation. It seemed to begin deep down inside my horse, gradually coming to the surface and spreading rapidly over his entire body. The vibration became so violent I could feel my knees pulsating against the saddle. The gray was standing like the Rock of Gibraltar but shaking like a leaf. Something had to be done quickly—right now! The grounds were coming alive with horse vans. Riders were mounting up. The Master was there, greeting friends and new members. The huntsman and hound truck would be along any minute now, and I had to get my horse under control before we moved out. When a horse freezes like that, you had better do something fast, because his next move could be an explosion.

I clucked, and the gray leaped forward. I swung him toward a far corner, hoping to work him down before the hunt got under way. He kept getting stronger and more erratic. The morning stillness was broken by the long wavering note of the huntsman's horn, and the field began moving north up Duhollow Road. I followed along, keeping well back—I was fighting for time. The gray horse was fighting for his head.

As we cut through the Dixon estate, the hounds were cast, and then the worst happened. They picked up the scent of a fox almost immediately and were off in full cry. The gray was bouncing in place like a huge pogo stick. Two latecomers passed me at full gallop, and that was it! For a moment I thought he was sitting down, and then with a mighty lunge and forward thrust of his head—almost jerking me out of the saddle—the gray sprang forward, then shot ahead with an acceleration that took my breath away. There was no holding him now!

I was still trying to regain my seat and haul in rein at the same time. The field was up ahead, but we were closing the distance with a rush. I set a pulley rein, heaving back with all my strength—what was left of it. I yelled, "Gangway ahead!" but the wind caught my words, flinging them back into my face. A stone wall loomed ahead. We passed over it as if it weren't there, then jumped two more in quick succession.

We hit the woods, flying. The trail made a sharp left, and there, right smack in front of us, stood the entire field. "W-h-o-o-o-o-a-a!" Two riders saw me coming and jumped clear. The third one, a girl on a black horse, didn't quite make it. We hit her—B-O-O-M! The gray grunted with the impact of our collision. The black horse was moving with the blow and didn't get the full force—but I did. The jarring halt spun me out of the saddle. I turned over once, landed on my feet, then my seat, and sat there still holding the reins.

When I got up, my trembling legs almost gave way. I tried mounting him again, but the gray refused to stand, backing, wheeling away. His eyes were white-rimmed, and his entire body was dark and slippery with sweat.

The hunt got under way, and he took off after them. I had one foot in the stirrup, with the rest of me barely hanging on; we must have covered two hundred yards before my saddle and breeches got together.

The remainder of the hunt went like the beginning. I didn't run down anyone else, but that wasn't my fault. By this time everybody gave me a wide berth. The nightmare raged on for two more endless hours.

As I grew weaker, the gray horse grew stronger. The end came in the Star Ridge area. We had just put a fox to ground, and it was a frustrated pack of hounds that hit a hot scent again on Star Ridge. The field split in two parts, and somehow I found myself on the tail end of the first section.

I was still battling my plunging gray horse, circling away whenever I got too close. I used any buffer I could run into—heavy brush, trees, anything I could find—to stem our onward drive. We were running through a long, narrow strip about fifty feet wide, heavily fenced on both sides by timber and barbed wire. There was no room to circle, and it was impossible to turn back with the second section hot on my heels. The only direction I could take was straight ahead. The going was downhill over rough, rocky terrain. If I checked too hard, the gray's head would come up, and at that pace he'd turn over with both of us, so I let him go.

They were slowing down up front and peeling off over a wooden coop. I roared, "Heads up! Heads up!" and came barreling right on through the middle. They scattered before me in a frantic effort to give me clearance, and as I shot by, their cries of indignation slammed against my ears.

We flew over the coop, passing Master, huntsman, and hounds. This is the worst breach of etiquette on the hunt field. I was too embarrassed to face them again, so I let the gray horse roll on, swinging toward home.

Gradually he came down to a trot, then a jog, then a walk. It really didn't matter anymore. I was numb with shame and limp with exhaustion. My hat was gone, my face was whipped raw by slashing brush, my coat sleeve was half torn off, and both hands were blistered through my gloves. This morning seemed a hundred years ago. I had been sure I had a thirty-five-hundred-dollar horse.

Right now I'd be lucky to get fifty bucks for him.

We met our cows on the road approaching the farm. Bill Uhlar was driving them. We plodded on past, and I was grateful Bill had the decency to keep his mouth shut.

I washed down the gray and walked him until he was cool. After a rubdown I put him in his stall and fed him. I said nothing to him, and he said nothing to me. I poured a bucket of cold water over my head, then sprawled out on a bale of hay and lay there a long time, staring up at the ceiling.

CHAPTER IV

IT TOOK THREE DAYS FOR MY BATTERED CONFIDENCE and beat-up bones to feel usable again. The gray hadn't fared too well, either. His body was a mass of nicks and scratches, and he had knocked off at least thirty pounds that showed in the quarters and tucked-up flanks.

Chris didn't say a word when I told him about our hunt, but in his eyes I could see the new tractor fading rapidly. However, I hadn't given up yet, not by a long shot.

The proper bit in the gray's mouth was the answer, one that would hold and control him in the hunt field. This was not as easy as it sounded, because a bit that works well for one horse might not work at all for another. The experiment would be simply a case of trial and error—and could be tested only in the hunting field. Alone, he was a cinch to ride, but in the company of other horses, especially when hounds were running, the gray horse was impossible. One more important element could not be overlooked: he might not have the temperament for hunting. But I would admit that only if nothing else worked.

Hounds met three times a week, and by the middle of September my tack room held such a conglomeration of bits and bridles that you would have thought I had a stable full of horses. I bought some and borrowed more—hackamore, wire snaffle, pelham, gag, kimberwick, and many others, in addition to a drop-nose band and martingales and combinations of all. I tried them out one at a time, but the results were always the same catastrophe on horseback. I was a glutton for punishment. My back developed a permanent ache, and many mornings I could hardly get out of bed. But I would not stop. There had to be an answer somewhere.

Chris saw me hobbling around one morning and seized the opportunity to confront me.

"You can't go on like this!" My brother's voice was stern. "What in the world are you trying to prove?"

"I'm not trying to prove anything!" I shot back. "I'm just not ready to give up, that's all!"

"You're not ready to give up! So what about me and the farm? You're supposed to be working here. You're supposed to be helping me!" The muscle on Chris's jaw began to ripple. He waited a moment to let his anger cool before he finished. "I'm handling this place all by myself, Mike, and by the looks of things I'm going to wind up taking care of you, too."

I backed off. He was right; this whole business had gotten away from the original purpose. The gray horse was no longer just a challenge to me. He was an obsession. He would not slow down, and I could not make him. I had assumed that he saved his dynamite strictly for the hunt field, but one night he showed me what a disaster he could be in the barn.

During the fox-hunting season in the colder climates most horses must be clipped for the outdoors and blanketed for the indoors. A sweating, long-coated horse in the hunting field is almost impossible to cool out and a surefire candidate for pneumonia.

Bill Uhlar was a good man with the clippers. After supper one evening we brought the gray out in front of his stall. I stood at his head, my hand on his halter shank. Bill switched on the electric clippers, and then the lid blew off! *Boom!* The gray's head struck the ceiling with such force that the barn shook. He reared back, slamming the wall, then came forward with his ears flat and his mouth wide open. He struck out in front, then lashed out behind, sending an empty bucket through a window.

The crash of exploding glass shot him forward against the feed bin.

It all happened so fast I failed to let go of the halter rope and went with him. He backed off with a grunt, then came around low and fast. This time I met him halfway, and the next thing I knew, I was spinning across the floor like a ballet dancer. I bounced off the hay chute and landed on the floor flat on my back. When I rolled to hands and knees, Bill was peeking out of the stall door, still holding the clippers with the broken cord hanging from it. The gray horse, all wall-eyed and bushy-tailed, was standing in the middle of the barn floor watching both of us.

Bill and I came together slow and easy and stood there talking things over. Bill repaired the clippers' cord and tried again. This time the machine was switched on in the far end of the room, and he came in quietly, giving the horse time to get used to it. Again the same explosion. He let the horse smell the instrument and tried again. No go. Feeding and crooning lullabies didn't work either. A twitch was applied to his upper lip to keep his mind off the clippers, but the results were even worse. By now we had a badly chewed-up floor, a broken window, and a cracked feed bin. It was a cold night, but half an hour after we began, the horse was so soaked with sweat it would have been impossible to clip him anyway. We called it off.

When the gray was calm enough and cool enough, we

put him away. As we left the barn, Bill said, "I guess he just doesn't want his hair cut." There's always a way, though; the next morning Doc Steiner shot the gray horse with a double tranquilizer and we clipped him.

That week was exceptionally mild. Then an icy wind came down out of the northwest, paralyzing everything in its path. Saturday was a moody kind of day, cloudy and cold but shot through by moments of sunshine and snow flurries. Hounds met at noon at Johnson's Corner, overlooking Peach Lake. We started out slowly, moving southeast with our backs to the wind, then swung in a wide arc coming up Dongle Ridge. A deer broke cover, bounding to the right, and then like magic a red fox appeared on a stone wall just ahead and vanished into the brush. There was a long pause as the hounds moved in his direction, then a high bugle note and full chorus. The chase was on.

I knew this country well; as soon as I established the direction the field was taking, I cut away from them, taking the long way and trying to keep them in sight at the same time. This was not the sporting thing to do, but by now I was devising ways to avoid trouble. The fox had plans of his own. He ran a two-mile circle, coming in my direction. He must have passed really close, but I never saw him. The gray horse and I came out of Merry's Woods, flying low, and cannonballed across the Murdock fields—down a slope, over a stone wall—and collided head-on with the entire field.

Thirty minutes later, after the third riderless horse had been rounded up, our Master rode up alongside me. I knew what was coming. His voice was low, but in no uncertain terms he ordered me from the field. The gray horse would never again hunt with the Goldens Bridge Hounds.

The battle of the hunting field had taken a lot out of both of us, physically and mentally. I continued to exercise my horse just enough to keep his condition up and spent most of the day working with Chris. He never again spoke to me about giving up. I guess he figured it would do no good.

I saw Jenny quite often during that time. She had gotten a job with Doc Steiner, handling his phone calls and billing his customers. She often dropped in at the farm after work, and we talked together more than we ever had before. She would also check with me on the meanings of horse terminology that customers used when they phoned. "Mike, someone called today, said his horse was off on the near front leg."

"Means the horse is lame on his left front leg. Near side of a horse is his left side," I explained, "off side is his right." Question: "I'm picking up my horse in the spring." Answer: "I'll start conditioning my horse in the spring, start exercising him." "My horse acts colicky" means he's got a bellyache.

These back-and-forth questions and answers brought us closer together. They also began giving me a more positive feeling about becoming a veterinarian. I'd often toyed with the idea, especially after I'd been around Doc Steiner, but of late it had really begun crystallizing in my mind.

"Mike, did you ever think about becoming a veterinarian?" Jenny asked one day, as we stood together watching the gray munch his evening grain.

"It's funny that you should ask me that, Jen," I answered. "Actually I've been giving it a lot of thought lately."

I reached out and stroked the gray's silky neck. "Since you've been working for Doc Steiner and since you've been asking me all that stuff about horses, I've come to realize how interested I am in veterinary medicine."

I paused to reflect on my words before I continued. "Jen, I can't tell you how often when I've been treating some sick animal I wished I knew more about what I was doing."

Jenny placed her hand on my arm, resting on the top of the stall door. I turned to face her.

"And I wish I knew more about training a horse!" I added quickly. "Look at this horse, Jen. Surely he's cut out for something more distinctive than a lone hack in the woods. He should be where people could see and admire him. He's an idiot in the hunt field, but he certainly can run and jump. There must be a place for him where he could show his abilities without fifty other horses running up his back."

That night, lying awake in bed, I thought perhaps his

destiny lay in the show ring. There were several more shows scheduled for that fall season, and I decided to try the Stamford one first.

I set up a small course of fences in one of our back fields. When I rode the gray over it, I found his pace even and controlled, and he jumped with such smooth, relaxed confidence that my lagging enthusiasm was fired all over again. This time we would make it!

Our entry fees had been paid, and two days before the show we trailered over to the Stamford show grounds for a schooling. I took the gray horse over every fence on the course separately, then in sequence. His round was fair, getting a little too strong toward the end, but nothing to worry about.

The day of the show we arrived at Stamford an hour before my first class. I had brought Jimmy Horgan, a thirteen-year-old neighbor, to help out. We unloaded at the parking area. Jimmy unbuckled the gray's sheet, while I unwrapped his legs and tacked him up. His head was up and curious, but there was no indication of nerves. So far so good. I mounted and walked confidently toward the show ring.

Our first class was Hunter Hack—walk, trot, canter, but no jumping. I had entered this class for warm-up and relaxation. We didn't expect a ribbon, and we didn't get one.

Over the loudspeaker: "Class number eight coming up, open working hunter over the outside course." We marked time in a large enclosure, with sixteen other riders, waiting for our number to be called.

"Number thirty-four next over the outside course!"

"That's for us, gray horse."

We broke smoothly and approached our first fence at a canter. It was an Aiken—a spread of brush with a rail on top. He jumped in stride and rolled on to the next, a coop—then a post-and-rail—and he was leveling off and beginning to move on too rapidly. "Slow down! Slow down!" It would look like the devil if I checked too hard, so I let him stride on, still trying to conceal his runaway. A Millbrook came at us too fast. He flattened out on top of the fence and rapped hard behind. He met a left turn like a polo pony on a ball, then really slipped into high gear. Most horses pick up pace heading toward home base, but the gray horse was flying. The rushing wind blurred my vision. Just ahead the white gate was hurtling toward us at an alarming rate. I guess I asked too soon, for the gray left the ground when he had at least two more strides to go. He struck the top of the gate so hard wood splinters exploded in all directions. His nose hit the turf, and for two heartbeats his quarters blotted out the sun as he catapulted on over.

I met the earth on my shoulder, then twisted sideways to get clear of him. I came to my feet as the gray struggled to his. There was a humming in my head, and I couldn't get my horse into focus. I reached out and steadied myself against his shoulder, with my head down to keep from passing out. A wave of nausea swept through me, and I got sick.

Somebody put me on my back with a cool wet towel across my forehead. I was glad Jenny wasn't present. An ambulance drove up; I was lifted into it. As we drove off, I couldn't see my gray horse anywhere.

They kept me in the hospital for several hours. I told them I was okay, that I had to get back, but they didn't release me until late afternoon.

Someone drove me back to the show grounds. They were deserted except for discarded programs and paper cups. The sun had already set, but a rosy afterglow enveloped the misty landscape.

Then suddenly I saw my trailer, and right in front of it the gray horse was peacefully grazing with Jimmy on the other end of the halter rope. After what had happened I don't know why I was so darned happy to see that horse.

On the way home Jimmy said, "Guess this isn't your lucky horse," but he was never more wrong.

CHAPTER V

I SET UP A TRAINING PROGRAM TO SLOW THE GRAY DOWN.
The bits hadn't worked, but maybe a cavaletti would. This
simple contraption was made of four parallel logs lying
flat on the ground four feet apart. I staked them to make
sure they wouldn't roll. When I first asked him to walk
through this arrangement, the gray horse flatly refused.
But after a little coaxing he finally did. Then we trotted
through. If he tried to canter, he'd get all tangled up and
almost fall on his face. He soon caught on, and within

three days he was negotiating the cavaletti like a dressage horse, all rhythm and balance.

Next I set up a small rail fence twelve feet beyond the last log. The first time I faced him into that fence, he took hold and tried to rush, but here was where the cavaletti went to work. It lay between him and the fence—and could only be trotted. The twelve feet beyond the last log gave him just enough room to get his hocks under him to jump. He tried to do it his own rushing way at first, but after half going down several times, he straightened out. We worked one week with the cavaletti and then without it. At last I was getting through to him.

We jumped fences from a trot all over the countryside. I constructed combination jumps, always varying the distance between them. He now began paying attention, sharpening up. He had always been a good jumper; now he was becoming a clever one, correcting his mistakes when he made them and never making the same one twice over the same fence.

But there was still one problem I couldn't solve. When jumping a course, he would increase his pace so alarmingly after the third fence that no judge could honestly give him a ribbon. A working hunter is judged on his way of going and safety in jumping. The gray horse did not look safe—and yet it never ceased to amaze me how well he could fence at high speed. I tried him in two more shows as a working hunter, and even though we were never pinned, he didn't take any more fences apart.

Then came the Goldens Bridge Show. Our schooling before this event was unexceptional but adequate. The course was a long U shape, moving counterclockwise. There were four obstacles on each side of the U but no fences on the curve. It seemed made to order for the gray horse and me. The sharp U turn would slow his pace, and a large pond bordering the outside of the curve would keep him lined up on course.

The day of the show was unbearably hot for October. Horses were dripping wet, tempers were short, and the soft-drink stand ran out of ice. I didn't gripe about the weather, though, just hoped it would knock some of the edge off my four-legged cyclone. When our number was called, we moved out quietly. Doc Steiner was the standby vet, and Jenny had come with him. This was going to be our moment of triumph. I'd show them how good my gray horse really was.

As expected, he opened up after the third fence, and one stride beyond the fourth I began holding him back for the turn. His throttle was wide-open now, and he was bulging too far to the right, but by this time we were two-thirds around and I was sure the pond would take him the rest of the way.

That was my mistake. Time and distance ran out. The water came skidding in on our right too fast and much too close. My right leg rammed against his ribs, pushing, driving him over. His nose was hauled around so far it jammed against my left knee; then with a sickening lurch the bank gave and dropped from under us. I turned his head loose, caught my breath, and for two beats he seemed to hang in space—then shot downward. His front legs locked in the mud, and he cartwheeled, dumping us both with a tremendous wallop.

I never felt the water—only the bottom. I got my legs under me and surfaced like a tuna taking a hook, then lost my balance and went under again. I came up in only three feet of water plus two feet of slimy muck. I dragged my loaded boots toward shore, falling, getting up, falling again. My hat floated by. I grabbed it and stuck it on my head. My horse was in up to his belly. He was all one color—dark, muddy green, including saddle and bridle, with some kind of greenish gook hanging from one ear.

I caught his rein and tried pulling him after me, but he was stuck. Somebody threw me one end of a rope. I slipped it around his stern, securing the loop with a bow-line knot against his chest. Then, with half a dozen men on the other end of the rope and a steward in the water behind the gray, splashing and shouting and waving his arms, we all staged a tug-of-war that lasted well over twenty minutes.

When the gray horse and I were finally landed, I was still too mad and embarrassed to thank anybody. I led him off the course and across the road to the trailer, put him in just the way he was, and drove home. I didn't see Jenny anywhere.

This was the end! I was through. This horse had

dropped me, dragged me, beaten me, and humiliated me all over Westchester and Putnam counties—and I had never complained and still had faith in him. But when this no-good misfit had tried to drown me, I quit!

I hardly looked at him for more than a week—just fed him and watered him. I ran an ad in the local paper, and the sooner I got rid of him the better. That was the way things stood when Derf came along.

The late afternoon of October tenth found me sitting on our front-porch steps eating an apple and watching the sun go down. I remember the date well because it marked the beginning of a new era for the gray horse and me— and even though what happened sounds like a movie, it really happened this way.

A dusty Plymouth station wagon with a Virginia plate stopped in our driveway, and a man wearing dark baggy slacks and a faded blue shirt stepped out and came limp-ing toward me. When I rose to meet him, I could see he was about my height, only thinner and older, with thick salt-and-pepper hair and hard gray eyes.

He said in a southern drawl, "Howdy, son. I'm Derf, the new man."

"Derf?" I asked.

The man smiled. "That's right."

I had almost forgotten that Chris had hired a new helper, but I shook his hand, pleased to meet him. We drove down to the barn, and I helped him unload two strapped suitcases and a beat-up footlocker, then stashed the whole works under the bed in the room next to the hayloft.

"I never heard of anyone named Derf." I ventured to break the awkward silence between us.

"My name was Fred," the man said in a matter-of-fact voice. "I didn't like it—too ordinary—so I changed it to Derf, Fred spelled backwards."

I nodded to indicate I could understand his feeling about Fred, but I really didn't.

It was nearly suppertime when we finished getting him settled, so we both started for the house to wash up. I was giving him a one-man rundown of the farm when suddenly Derf froze in his tracks, staring intently at my horse grazing along the fence. Without so much as a by-your-leave he left me standing there with my mouth open and made straight for the pasture and the gray horse. He ducked under the top rail, and the gray's head came half-way up, watching his approach with pricked ears and questioning nostrils.

When they were six feet apart, both became a piece of sculpture, silhouetted against the red-and-gold trees as if they'd been there forever, and for nearly a minute it seemed that time stood still and not a leaf rustled or a bird chirped.

Derf said something to the gray horse and moved in closer, running his fingers down the shoulder and that thin, jagged scar. He stepped back and walked around the horse, speaking softly; then he came up slowly to the gray's head. With one hand he grasped the halter while the other explored the inside of the soft upper lip.

I came up quietly and leaned my elbows on the barway. Though I was puzzled, I didn't say a word.

When Derf turned to me again, there was a strange unbelieving look in his eyes. "I know this horse!" The words came slowly, as if he'd been hypnotized. "Never thought I'd see him again—but there can be no mistake—same registration number under his lip, same scar, same look." His eyes were distant as he gently placed his hand on the scarred shoulder. "Third fence—Maryland Cup Race, '76. I was on him when he got this and under him when I got mine."

Nettie outdid herself that night. Derf was a new face at the table, and she set out to impress him with her cooking. A huge bowl of green salad was already in the center of the table when we sat down to dinner. And minutes later Nettie came bustling in with a steaming platter of lamb garnished with steamed onions and mushrooms. Then came baked potatoes and green peas. There was little conversation at the table except for Nettie's account of the numerous small catastrophes that had befallen her relatives. After the dessert of ice cream and fresh-baked chocolate chip cookies, we walked into the living room, carrying our cups of coffee. Nettie followed with the pot and set it down on the coffee table.

All I kept thinking about was the gray horse and how much I wanted to know about him. At last after a suitable silence I said, "Derf, please tell me about my horse. So far I haven't had much luck with him. He's too hot to hunt, and he won't show. What can he do? What did he do?"

"Race, my friend!" Derf's answer came almost before I finished my question.

We sat in the living room until way past midnight, listening to Derf unfold the story of the gray horse. Nettie settled back in the armchair by the fireplace. But Chris, who never seemed to be interested in anything but dairy farming and baseball, balanced on the edge of his chair like a child at a movie. His eyes were glued on Derf, and he hardly moved a muscle through the entire telling of the story.

"As a three-year-old," Derf began, "that gray was the best darned timber-horse prospect in the whole state of Virginia—and let me tell you, there were some great ones out that year. I was riding for Jon Whitcomb when this green colt joined us. Irish thoroughbred he was, name of Viking, by Norway King out of that great jumping mare Blythebourne. From the very beginning this youngster had it. You know, some horses are fair athletes and some are good athletes—but this ball of fire was a great one.

"He went to work like he'd had ten years' experience behind him—and, brother, that colt could run and jump with the best of them!

"I started him—meaning I brought him along slow and easy—but the son of a gun was so loaded with talent there was no stopping him. When you get a colt like that, one that can really move on and jump big, you sometimes forget that he's only a baby with more talent than know-how, and you push him ahead too fast and make him do a lot of things he's not ready for.

"I guess that's what happened to Viking—and I have no one to blame but myself. You let most horses get a couple of seasons of hunting under their belt before you start racing them over timber. You've got to give them a chance to learn about bad going and trappy fences before you start pouring it on—but I began racing Viking the same year I broke him."

As the clock ticked away and the crackling fire gradually became a bed of glowing embers, I rode in "point-to-points" and "steeplechases," galloping beside great riders and all the great horses that went with them. It was a tale of action—a galaxy of thrills and spills. The room became more and more charged as we sensed the climax. A dog barked somewhere in the night, and from faroff came the lonely wail of the 12:45 out of Brewster.

Derf leaned back, lit a cigarette, and his next words came bitterly through a thick haze of swirling blue smoke.

"The Maryland Hunt Cup is the toughest, most spectacular timber race in the country. It began as a local hunter race but has gradually grown to a leading sporting event of national and even world significance. The great rider Noel Laing once said that he would look forward with pleasure to another ride in the Grand National at Aintree but shuddered at the thought of riding in the Maryland Hunt Cup again. He knew what he was talking about. I've ridden Aintree myself—twice, to be exact—and got around both times, but I made three tries at Maryland and never finished once. I was coming up for my fourth go-around on Viking and figured this time, with this great horse, I'd make it.

"It had rained hard the day before and all through the morning of the big race, and even though the sun came out in the afternoon, at racetime the turf was still slick. There were nine in the field, and when the flag dropped at the starting line, you'd have thought we had a fast track at Belmont in front of us. Fences one and two went by like a shot, and we were still bunched pretty close as we drove into the third.

"Sundance hooked timber—turned over. Boomerang, riding his tail, came right down on top of him. It all happened like a stroke of lightning—crash—*boom!* I checked the gray horse and slid in too close, then tried too late. The top rail ripped loose—came with us—and the last thing I remembered was a rider's crash helmet spinning up in front of me. It spun a long time against a hazy gray backdrop, then slowed down and reversed, and as it stopped for the second time I could hear a woman's voice coming from a great distance. I opened my eyes to a white

ceiling and a white-capped nurse. 'How do you feel?' she
asked.

"How did I feel? One arm and both legs were suspended from pulleys, and one great big headache was
throbbing through the rest of me. I'd been in the hospital for five lost days, but eight more weeks passed before
I hobbled out on a pair of crutches. I knew I would never
ride again, but I had to find out what happened to the
gray horse. I heard Whitcomb sent him to Philadelphia.
I visited him there at the Veterinarians' Clinic, where they
were still trying to repair his mutilated shoulder. When
I left, I knew his riding days were over, too, and I was
sure I'd never see him again."

Derf paused and stared at the glowing hearth. Then
he said, "A whole year went by before I was strong enough
to take a manager's job at a small riding academy in New
Jersey. I got fired—and went on to another job, then another, downhill all the way. Guess the gray's luck ran the
same course—passing from one stable to the next, never
finding his place, and always getting farther and farther
away from it. When I read your ad in the *Chronicle*, I
figured cows might be a good change for me. I grew up
on a dairy farm, so I wasn't exactly inexperienced."

The room was dark now. Derf stretched his legs, and
his thin face shone for a moment as he lit another cigarette. He rose to leave, but at the door he turned, looking straight at me. "Son," he said, "I've known a lot of
horses in my time—good ones, bad ones, lazy ones, ea-

ger ones—all kinds—just like people, only more direct and less complicated. But that Viking was one of the best horses that ever looked through a bridle, and I'll never forget him."

I accompanied Derf down to the barn and said good night, then went below for my nightly bed check. When the lights came on, the gray's head came over the stall door, his eyes blinking in the harsh brightness. Impulsively I slipped an arm over his neck and pressed my face against his cheek. Never again would he be just the gray horse. He was Viking, who had had a great future and lost it at the third fence at the Maryland Hunt Cup—and I was the stupid kid with all the answers, the know-it-all who frustrated him every inch of the way, always trying to turn him into something he wasn't. The pieces fit now: the scar, the timber fences, and his great talent to run and jump. The mystery of the gray horse was solved. I turned off the lights and walked slowly up to the house. My mind was whirling.

CHAPTER VI

THREE NIGHTS LATER I CORNERED DERF IN HIS ROOM. I had been trying to catch him alone for three days, but he always seemed to be tied up with one thing or another, as if he knew what I had on my mind and wanted no part of it.

I went up the back stairs of the barn two at a time, banged once on the door, and barged right in. Derf was lying on his bed reading a magazine. Before I could get my mouth open, he got the first word in: "Nothing doing, kid—you can't race that horse again 'cause it wouldn't work. Now forget it and be a good boy and leave me alone."

"Why wouldn't it work?" I countered. "Tell me why it wouldn't work and I'll lay off."

I stood there in the middle of the room breathing hard, waiting, and Derf calmly lit a cigarette before he spoke.

"It wouldn't work because any fool knows you can never go back. It wouldn't work because the gray horse has had it and so have I, and even if he could still run and jump, who in blazes would ride him?"

"I can ride him," I shot back at him, and as I caught his condescending smile, I drove on. "You don't know what kind of a rider I am—how could you when you never even saw me on a horse? I'm not the fancy kind you were, but I've been on horses all my life. I've trained hunters and jumpers and showed some real tough ones, too, so I'm not exactly a greenhorn, and what I don't know you can teach me. And as far as the gray horse is concerned, I'll bet you he's as good now as he ever was—maybe better. You said yourself that a horse needs experience before he can be raced over timber. Well, he's had experience! Four or five years of it, not counting the time he's had with me. He knows about bad going and trappy fences and all the rest of it. All he needs now is someone to give him a break and let him go on and do what he was born for." I stopped to catch my breath, then went on more slowly, pleading. "Don't you see, Derf, you fixed his wagon in the beginning and I goofed him up plenty in the middle. Why can't we both get together now and square things up with him and with ourselves? Tell me, is that asking too much?"

Derf lay silent while I spoke, yet somehow I knew I was reaching him. His eyes were fixed straight ahead, and the cigarette lay idle in his fingers. When I finished, he sat up and looked at me a long time. He took another drag on his cigarette, then methodically pressed it out, picked up his magazine, and dropped back on the pillow.

"Okay, kid, we'll see what you can do tomorrow. Good night."

I walked out of the room. At the door I turned and said, "Thanks, Derf." If he heard me, he never let on. He just lay there staring up at the ceiling.

The next morning, after the cows had been milked and fed, I tacked up Viking and rode out to meet Derf at the ring. When I had disclosed my plans to Chris, I had expected a battle, but much to my surprise he went right along. He would hire Bill Uhlar to help bear the work load so that Derf could spend more time with the gray horse and me. All his life Chris had been a hardworking, hardheaded stick-in-the-mud, but Derf had sparked him, too, and right now if this was what I wanted, Chris would back me all the way.

Derf had already arrived at the ring and was standing in the middle of it, puffing on a cigarette. I went through the barway and right to work. Walk—trot—stop—back. Viking was on his toes after his long layoff, but like most thoroughbreds I had known, he began quietly and got stronger—blew up once or twice, then settled down and paid attention. I warmed up with him. We cantered and changed leads, then hand-galloped. We came up the side of the ring and jumped a post-and-rail and coop, then turned and came back over them. Every now and again I glanced over at Derf, but his expression was poker-faced and I could learn nothing from it. After the last fence I pulled up in front of him and waited. I thought we had performed well, but Derf's words quickly punctured my balloon.

"Well, you don't have any real bad habits, but you've sure got a lot to learn." He paused to let the rest of the air run out, then continued. "First, when you drive a car, do you look at the radiator hood while you're making a turn, or look down for your gas and brake when you need them? No! You look where you're going all the time, right? It's the same thing on a horse. Remember, the eyes are one of the most important controls a rider has, but he has to use them correctly. He must never look at the horse's head or down at his hands when he's riding to win. When you're going into a turn, bring your eyes around the turn first, and the horse will follow. If you don't, you'll meet it too suddenly and either cut too close or swing too wide. And as far as jumping goes, the eyes work in a slightly different way. You've got to keep them up—straight ahead—and see your fence only in the perimeter of your vision, without looking directly at it. The moment you don't do this, timing goes off and no good comes of it. With any good race rider all this is basic. If you're going to race that good gray horse over timber, it's got to be that way with you, too."

I followed and nodded with every word he spoke, but I must have looked more than a little deflated because Derf smiled and added, "Son, I know this is a lot of stuff to throw at a guy all at once, but you're young, your reflexes are good, and I think maybe you can do it. It won't be easy, not by a long shot, but remember, you asked for it."

I asked for it, all right—and got it too. Even though I had been on and off horses since childhood I was strictly a seat-of-the-pants rider—a hit-and-miss one who learned the hard way, which is not always the best way. I rode instinctively with no true knowledge or understanding, just guts and energy and a seemingly indestructible ego.

The very week I began working my horse under Derf's supervision, an unusual thing happened that triggered an important decision. I was at home alone watching the late show on TV. Nettie had gone off to visit a cousin. Chris was at a local meeting of dairy farmers.

"Don't forget to keep an eye on Marge," Chris reminded me. "Her calf is overdue. I don't want anything to go wrong." As he went out the door, he added, "Doc Steiner said he'd come by later."

Just before nine o'clock I strolled down to the barn to check things out. The night was chilly, and as I approached the barn a large orange moon was coming up over the roof. When I had gone to see the cow only an hour before, Marge had been standing quietly, but now as I entered the barn I heard a loud groaning sound coming from her stall. When I got there, Marge was flat on her side. Her body, dark with sweat, was sending up a thick steamy vapor into the cold night air. Her flanks were heaving spasmodically, and when I knelt by her side, her head swung toward me. She was in agony.

I sprang to my feet, uncertain what to do next, but suddenly in the glow of the overhead light I saw the calf. It was almost one-third of the way out. Only the head and one leg were visible. The other leg must be folded back, still inside her body. Something had to be done right now. She could not possibly give birth unless the head and both legs came out together.

I recalled once watching Doc Steiner handle a situation like this with a foal. How different could it be with a calf? Don't just stand there, Mike—move! I rushed down the alleyway to the sink at the far end. I peeled off my jacket, rolled up my shirt sleeves, and scrubbed my hands vigorously with soap and hot water—then charged back to Marge. Rubber gloves would be better, but my bare hands would have to do. I reached out and grasped with both hands as much of the calf as I could see. If I pulled, the bent leg would tear the cow apart, so I pushed, never letting go of the calf. It did not go back easily, for Marge was pushing in the opposite direction.

At last I was inside the cow up to my elbows, feeling frantically for the bent leg. When I found it, I brought it carefully up alongside of the other, then pulled the calf slowly toward me. Marge groaned. "Hold on, girl, we'll be home free in a minute."

Sweat was pouring down my forehead, blinding me. I could feel my shirt plastered against my back. My breath was coming in short grunts. Suddenly I was down in the damp straw with the calf in my arms.

"We did it, Marge!" I cried out. The cow labored to her feet, and I rolled away from the newborn, completely exhausted.

I don't know how long I lay there. I might have fallen asleep. All of a sudden I looked up and saw Doc Steiner standing over me. The calf was struggling to rise, and Marge was trying to lick it dry.

"What happened here?" Doc asked.

I felt chilled as I climbed to my feet. Doc Steiner handed me my jacket. I described what had taken place as I zipped it up.

"You did it just right, Mike," he said as he slapped me on the shoulder. "I couldn't have done better myself."

I was in a sort of daze as I walked back to the house. This had been a life-or-death emergency, and I, Mike Benson, had handled it just right. Slowly the impact of what had happened in that barn crept over me. The elation I experienced was indescribable. Never in life had I known such a thrill of accomplishment. Never had I felt so alive—so wonderful!

The very next morning I sent in my application to the agricultural school at Cornell University in the hope of becoming a veterinarian—my mind was made up.

Of course, Chris was pleased. "First thing you've done that makes any sense," he declared, then added with a smile, "Mom and Pop would have been very happy."

I went to see Jenny to tell her about my new venture and my plan to race Viking in the Maryland Hunt Cup. She was delighted about Cornell but not about the Hunt Cup.

"Mike, are you sure you want to do this?" Her voice was anxious. "I know you've ridden horses all your life, but racing is different and dangerous, especially steeple-chasing—"

"But Derf is training me," I interrupted. "He feels I can do it. I've got the horse that certainly can. I want him to realize his potential."

"Mike," she pleaded, "you know it doesn't make any difference to Viking. He'd just as soon go on with the way things are. He doesn't—"

"But *I* want to do it!" I cut in hotly. "I want to see if I can. For the first time in my life I have a top horse. He's not a hack or a show horse or a hunter. He's a racehorse, bred to run." I stopped and groped for the right words. "Don't you see, Jenny, I want to do this for him *and* for me!"

I rose from the couch where we had been sitting. "I guess I'd better be going," I mumbled.

As I reached the door, I felt Jenny's restraining hand

on my arm. "Don't be angry, Mike." When I faced her, she reached up and kissed me lightly on the cheek. "Don't you see, I'm on your side," she said softly. "I just don't want to see you get hurt." As I drove home, I could still feel the warmth of her kiss.

There was no doubt that at this point Viking knew a great deal more about timber racing than I did, but Derf set up a concentrated training program in an all-out attempt to even up horse and rider. Now we both knew that Viking must return to Worthington Valley. Our target was the last Saturday in April and the Maryland Hunt Cup Race, and from now on our road was narrow and one way—with no room to turn back.

CHAPTER VII

VIKING SEEMED TO SENSE THE CHANGE, THE CHAL-
lenge, and rose to meet it like the thoroughbred he was.
We were playing for keeps now, with no time for she-
nanigans and horseplay, only hard work. But we could
not expect him to carry the full load of my schooling. I
leased an extra horse from Clark's stable and through the
following weeks ran a continuous two-horse relay team
with only one rider.

Chris hired Bill Uhlar full time, for Derf was spending
so much of the day with Viking and me. The extra

horse also added to the farm expenses.

"I'm drawing on Mom and Dad's insurance money to meet the additional bills," Chris confided in me one evening as we sat at the table after dinner. I felt bad about that, but I knew it had to be coming from somewhere.

Chris laid his hand on my shoulder. "Now don't feel guilty, Mike." He paused. "You know I never wanted to do anything but dairy farming. But you have an opportunity that comes once in a lifetime, so take it, brother. I'm behind you all the way."

Viking and I were drilled on basic dressage—pivots, two-tracks, and balancing exercises of all kinds—always aimed toward one goal: a winning combination of horse and rider.

Derf worked on my timing and coordination. A single post-and-rail was set up in the center of the ring, and we were taught to jump at a diagonal, coming at our fence from any direction. I knew that a straight line is the shortest distance between two points, but Derf gave it new meaning. "Remember, Mike," he'd repeat over and over, "as you approach a fence, establish an imaginary line between you and it and beyond, and ride that line all the way! Deviate and you'll throw your horse off balance at the most crucial moment—understand? Also, line up your fences so you can meet them in stride with no wasted motion. This is one of the major faults of green race riders—they waste time. Many a race has been lost because the jockey made a turn too wide or jumped one fence without considering the location of the next."

He hammered at me continuously, never letting up—just drive, drive, drive. When I goofed, he bawled me out, and when I was right, he didn't say a word. He was a tough taskmaster, but he understood me as well as he did Viking. He knew when I had had enough. He asked for supreme effort but always understood my limitations and never pushed me beyond them.

I questioned him only once. There was a three-week period when we worked only on the flat with no jumping. "Derf," I asked, "how come all this flat work when we're heading for a timber race?"

"How come?" he lashed back at me. "Because most of the trouble a guy gets into over a jump course comes from bad riding, not bad fencing. I can make a jump rider in three months, but it takes ten years to make a rider!"

I kept my mouth shut after that and did what I was told.

One morning Derf set up a series of small fences. My reins were tied up, and I jumped them in sequence with my hands behind my back or over my head. I was working on body position now—learning to be with my horse at all times without the use of reins for balance. Here again the eyes were extremely important. At times when Viking got in wrong and took a sticky one or stumbled badly, I found myself grabbing leather to stay aloft, but when my eyes were fixed on a point straight ahead and never looked down, no matter what, the problem solved itself, and my equilibrium held fast from start to finish.

Another exercise included the same series of jumps, only this time I galloped alongside and at a given signal from Derf swung in on a diagonal line, taking whichever one he designated.

"Pace! Pace! Pace!" Derf roared at me if I took a course or fences too fast or too slow. "Remember, Mike, you've got to have a stopwatch in your head that comes from your knees, and you've got to know what your horse feels every second he's under you. You must be able to foresee when he's right or wrong for a fence three or four strides away, then do something about it. When he's right, leave him alone, and if he's wrong, increase his stride, but at this point never shorten it. Okay? Now, let's try that again, Mike. And for Pete's sake, when you get into trouble, don't just sit there like a dummy—do something, anything, but don't just sit there."

I put everything I had into my job, and most of the time I felt it wasn't enough. I was striving for split-second reflex and coordination—the ability to think and do on a single flashing thought wave and never fumble in the process.

Even at night, lying in bed, I was still riding—trying. I'd fall asleep, then suddenly come awake with a start as my horse cut a turn or stumbled and went down. But next morning I was out there again, eager for what lay ahead. We were getting there, slowly but surely. I had good days and bad days, but as time went by, the bad ones became fewer.

My respect for and confidence in Derf grew with every hour, and at the end of three months I would have jumped the moon if he'd asked me. He had changed considerably. Most of his bitterness about the past was gone, and he talked a lot about the future. But on December evenings in front of the fire Chris and I liked to listen to him reminisce about the past. I couldn't get enough of the Maryland Hunt Cup and all the great horses that had run in it from its beginning in 1894 to the race as it was today. Time was when a good honest half-bred hunter with heart and a big jump in him could enter the Maryland with some hope of success. Today it had to be a thoroughbred, well built, capable of staying four miles, running all the way, and experienced at jumping big solid timber fences.

The difference between the past and present was pace. There was Billy Barton, one of the greatest, who captured the Hunt Cup three years in a row. He raced over his fences at great speed and jumped with incredible power. At one time the distance between his takeoff tracks and landing tracks was measured at thirty-three feet. There was Captain Kettle and Winton, and Ben Nevis II who broke the course record with a time of 8:33⅗ minutes, which still stands. The great Blockade won the Maryland three times, but fell and broke his neck in the Virginia Gold Cup of '42. And there was Noel Laing's Troublemaker, who died on the seventeenth fence and was buried there. There was Peterski, Jester's Moon, Third Army—an endless flow of great horses, and top riders like

Fred Colwill, Charles Fenwick, Jr., Stuart Janey, Mike Smithwick, and Joy Slater, who in 1981 was the first woman in sports history to win the Maryland Hunt Cup.

I learned about the course itself and the personality of its fences—the horse-killing third; the formidable sixth and sixteenth, standing side by side on the top of a hill; and the thirteenth, nicknamed "Union Memorial" after the Baltimore hospital of the same name.

The entire picture, filled with color and tremendous challenge, fired my imagination and made me feel capable of great things. Yet somehow, in the middle of it all, fear brushed lightly over me, and I wavered and wondered if I could measure up.

Shortly after Christmas winter struck in earnest. The ground became as hard as concrete, with three feet of snow on top that made riding impossible. We vanned Viking to an indoor ring near Bedford and there managed to keep him fit.

During this time I barely had a chance to see Jenny. We talked frequently over the phone and met occasionally when she came over to watch me work Viking.

"This isn't much fun for you, is it, Jen?" I asked one evening. We were walking together around the frigid indoor ring, leading Viking to cool him out after a hard workout. Jenny didn't answer. She seemed thoughtful and preoccupied. I stopped and took her hand. "I'll make it up to you, Jen," I promised. "When this is over I'll . . ."

Jenny placed her fingers against my lips. "Now don't

say anything you'll regret." She laughed. "I understand—don't worry about me. Now let's keep moving before Viking gets a chill."

I helped out on the farm whenever I had enough energy left to do so. One night while I was talking with Jenny, I fell asleep and woke to find she had placed a pillow under my head and covered me with an afghan.

When March was almost half over, my racing colors arrived. They had been registered and okayed by the National Steeplechase and Hunt Association and came in a brown-paper package from Miller Harness Company. It contained red cap and shirt with white blocks on the sleeves, white nylon pants—and one Caliente crash helmet. I tried them on in the barn.

"Well, Mike, looks like you're all ready to start." Derf's voice startled me as he came up behind and slapped me lightly on the shoulder. I nodded—but was it excitement or fear that made my throat so tight?

That evening after supper Derf leaned back in his chair with his hands locked behind his neck. He cleared his throat before he spoke. "Folks, I think it's about time we got this show on the road. I think maybe we ought to head this one-horse outfit down Virginia way and let Mike get a few hunt races under his belt before we hit the big one."

"Okay, you're the coach," Chris said. I nodded in agreement, for I knew the time had come to move on.

Just one week later we hit the trail south. The bed of

our pickup carried two suitcases, a tack trunk, two bales of hay, and half a sack of grain, all covered by a tarpaulin. I led Viking into the trailer about four-thirty in the morning, when we were ready to pull out. He loaded eagerly, then stood quietly, waiting to go.

I didn't feel quite as brave this morning as I had the night before. Jenny had come over to have supper with us, and our house had been warm with the aroma of good food and animated talk.

Just before dessert Nettie came marching into the room carrying a magnificent birthday cake. The burning candles, rising above the thick icing, flickered as Nettie and full chorus sang "Happy Birthday." What a surprise!

"This is a pre-birthday party," Jenny announced. "We won't all be with you on your birthday, so we're having the party right now!"

Then they all sang "For He's a Jolly Good Fellow," and followed it up with "Speech! Speech!"

When I got to my feet, I couldn't speak—my throat locked the words in. Jenny kissed me with feeling, and Nettie hugged me so hard I gasped for air. She passed me to Chris for the same treatment, while Derf practically shook my arm off.

Afterward I drove Jenny home. At her door I kissed her good night and held her in my arms. We didn't speak, for there was nothing more to say.

Now, before dawn, the air was raw and black, with a light snow falling straight down. Derf started the motor.

Chris walked me to the cab. His face looked drawn and anxious in the half-light as he squeezed my hand and said, too lightly, "Take care, Mike." The truck swung out of the driveway, and for some reason I was shaking.

CHAPTER VIII

I RAN MY FIRST RACE BETWEEN FLAGS AT STONY BROOK course in Southern Pines, North Carolina. The date was March 26, one day after my eighteenth birthday and exactly thirty-five days before the running of the Maryland Hunt Cup. There were twelve entries and a thousand-dollar purse, and the course was two and one-quarter miles over timber.

Derf gave me a full set of instructions before the start. "Now look, Mike, the course is fast, but if you let your horse run all-out, he'll flatten too much on top of his jumps. Rate him back and let the leaders do the wood-chopping. Keep a good feel of him, don't diddle at your fences, and you'll both come home together.

"Remember, Mike, this is your first race, so just give Viking a good ride and don't try to be a hero."

I wasn't as nervous as I'd thought I'd be—just loss of appetite and a touchy gut—but when the flag dropped and we winged over our first fence, the butterflies disappeared. Viking ran well and jumped big. One thing I learned right away: what was considered too fast a pace in the show ring was not fast enough down here. As soon as Viking realized I was leaving him alone, he became soft in my hands and came back or moved out at my fingertips. I followed Derf's orders but made my final bid too late—because six other guys moved at the same time. I wasn't sharp enough or fast enough to get position and got shoved way over to the outside. We swept across the finish line in seventh place, but Viking was still going strong, with room to spare. It was a good race with no time to fret or worry about anything.

That night Derf and I celebrated my initiation in a diner on Route 211. The food tasted better than it was. There was nothing wrong with my appetite now. We didn't rehash the race too much. We both knew that I had goofed at the finish, so there was no sense rubbing it in. Derf seemed satisfied with my ride, for with him no comment usually meant approval. It might also mean, "What's the use?"

We laid over in Southern Pines about ten days. Viking was put up in a small stable, and I worked him just enough to keep his condition up. Then we moved north on 301 and arrived in Richmond two days before the twenty-seventh running of the Deep Run Hunt Cup. We pulled into the stable area just before sundown. Entry fees had already been taken care of, and Viking's accommodations were ready, for Derf, a master of detail, operated like an advance-guard liaison.

We rented a room in a motel nearby, and while Derf showered I put through a call to Chris. One cow had died and six new calves had been born. I also called Jenny. She said that Marty and Wendy sent their best. And when she told me she was hoping to come down for the big race, I felt great.

The Deep Run Hunt Cup was run on Saturday, April ninth. Besides Viking, the field included five other timber-toppers—all first-rate—with riders to match. The course was three miles over eighteen timber fences. The day was sunny, warm, and the track was fast. We got off to a good start, and even though Viking ran and jumped with great ease, somehow we were skillfully outmaneuvered by our competition and lost ground continuously, especially on the turns. There were no falls, but when the six of us crossed the finish line, I was neck and neck with the last horse.

I couldn't understand what had gone wrong. So far as

I could see, neither one of us had fouled up, yet I couldn't help but wonder what Viking might have done with a decent rider on his back. Sometimes a good horse will make a fair rider look good, but a bad rider can always mess up a good horse. For the first time I asked myself what the heck I was doing down here.

Derf put Viking away and rubbed him down without a word. But outside the stall he pulled me down beside him on a bale of hay. I expected the ax, but instead he placed a hand on my shoulder and spoke softly.

"Don't feel so bad, Mike. You did all right. Your hands, seat, legs, everything check out okay. The only thing I can fault is your eyes. You keep them up off your fences, but in between you don't look where you're going. Yesterday I sent in our entry fee for the Maryland Hunt Cup, so we want to be sure we're in top shape when we get there. Now, Mike, I'll tell you what we're going to do. Our next race is the Little Grand National in Maryland. That gives us fourteen days, and from now till then we'll work on two points: your eyes—both of them— okay?"

That evening I wrote a long letter to Jenny. I described the race and what my coach had to say about it. Derf was stretched out on the bed reading a magazine. I recalled the night when I had barged into his room. Maybe he'd been right when he'd told me to forget about racing Viking. I don't think he ever regretted his final decision, though, and at this moment I didn't either.

The place for the running of the three-mile Grand National Point-to-Point was Western Run Valley, north of Baltimore. The weather was cloudy, cool, wet, and the time was Saturday, April twenty-third, just seven days this side of the Maryland Hunt Cup. Viking was in top shape, and I was just as fit—and raring to go.

Derf had drilled me mercilessly for the preceding two weeks. He had arranged a flat course between flags over a fifty-acre stretch of country near Warrenton, Virginia, and there, with the help of two sparring partners and an extra horse, I put in two hours a day of simulated racing conditions. I went over the course again and again, with the two riders continuously trying to trip me up. They used every trick in the book, plus a few extra, and after fourteen days of it I could weave through them like a broken-field runner. Right now not even gray skies or a slick track could dampen my confidence.

Because of the rain and trappy going, only seven of the original ten entries cantered up to the starting line. Gunhill, the favorite and a veteran of twenty-eight race meets, was the horse to beat. We got away smoothly and crossed the first eight fences in a sort of flying-wedge formation, with me somewhere in the middle and Gunhill running easily up front. I set my sights on him but never lost track of what was happening on either side. Two horses went down together on the tenth, and from there on in it looked like smooth sailing. There were eighteen fences in all, and after the sixteenth I was in the clear with only Gunhill two lengths ahead. A fierce kind of exhilaration gripped me. It was in the bag!

Nobody rode my flanks, and Viking closed the gap in a rush. We drove into the seventeenth a half length behind. Suddenly a tiny voice of warning began shouting in my ear, "Not yet! Take back! Take back!" But I wouldn't listen.

Gunhill jumped and triggered Viking into simultaneous flight. Gunhill was right for the fence, but Viking was too far back and lost altitude too soon. He dove at the top rail, his knees reaching for his chin and his quarters twisting sideways in a desperate bid for clearance. The crack of timber dropped his head out of sight as the rest of him came on over like a whiplash, propelling me straight out. The earth zoomed up and came down on the back of my shoulders, then flipped over half a dozen times and stopped on my face. The air vibrated with the thunder of hoofs and flying mud. I half rose to get out of there, but somebody shouted, "Lie still, you fool," as a horse and rider passed over.

When I finally lurched to my feet, the first thing I saw was Viking. His bridle had come off and was hanging between his forelegs, suspended by the rein, which was still looped over his neck. His muddy knees were shaking and his wet flanks heaving like a huge bellows. I took hold of the rein and led him from the field of battle. He was still stunned but seemed to move out okay.

What a bright boy I had turned out to be—a Class C

rider but a Class A dope. I couldn't wait until the stretch. I had to be a hero! But I guess I was still just a smart-aleck kid with a pinhead brain—and right now the same amount of heart.

As we wended our way through the crowd, I heard someone say, "Thought he broke his neck for sure!"

Next morning we pulled out of Butler, Maryland, and turned south toward Worthington Valley and the Maryland Hunt Cup. We drove slowly in a steady downpour. Derf was at the wheel, and I sat hunched in the opposite corner, staring out the window and listening to the rain beat against the windshield.

Viking had gone off his feed last night, but he had seemed all right this morning when we loaded him. There was a grinding ache in my neck and shoulders that racked my body with every bump in the road, and Derf's stillness didn't help my morale one bit.

"You know what happened out there yesterday, Mike, don't you?"

Derf's voice came sharply above the din of the motor and driving rain. I didn't answer, and Derf went on.

"Gunhill outfoxed you. His rider, Al Mead, is one of the finest jockeys in steeplechasing. He knew you were closing on him, so he regulated his pace and actually set you up for what happened." Derf never took his eyes off the road as he spoke. "I've seen Al Mead pull that stunt on better riders than you, so don't let it get to you. Just be a little more careful next time." At this point I began to wonder if there would be a next time.

The line fences that we passed along the road were the same kind I would face next Saturday. They looked big, grim, and indestructible with the rain dripping down from one solid pole to the next, then losing itself in green turf and gray pools of water.

I had awakened this morning with a black premonition of what lay ahead. The sight of these formidable structures shook my already crumbling confidence.

We stabled Viking at the Green Spring Valley Kennels in Glyndon, then found ourselves a motel just around the corner. I swallowed two aspirins, flopped down on the bed just the way I was, and slept fitfully all afternoon. When I awoke about four o'clock, my shoes had been removed and a light blanket had been thrown over me.

Derf was sitting at the desk across the room reading a newspaper. He looked up and smiled when he saw I was awake. "How do you feel?" he asked. I shrugged and smiled back, and Derf got to his feet and lit a cigarette. "Let's go out and get something to eat," he suggested.

When we stepped outside, the rain had stopped. A gray mist hung over the earth, but the sun was trying to break through. I took the wheel, and Derf slid in beside me. "Good boy," he said, and suddenly I felt much better.

The following afternoon I tacked up Viking for his first workout in this neck of the woods. The sun had come up shining bright, and I gave it the morning to dry up the aftermath of yesterday's deluge. The going was boggy in the low spots, but up on the hill above the stable the footing was pretty fair.

I worked Viking slowly for almost an hour, feeling him out for any aftereffects of our Grand National catastrophe. We had just popped a brush and two small fences when Derf drove up in the pickup. "How's he going?" he called out the window. I gave him a big grin with the high sign, pulling up beside the truck. "That's fine." He grinned back. "I'll meet you in that meadow north of the stable and watch you school over some real timber."

When I trotted into the field, Derf was already there. His back was to me with both hands resting on the top rail of a solid line fence almost as tall as he was. As I angled toward him, he spoke over his shoulder. "This fence measures about four foot three. It's the average fence you'll find over the Maryland Hunt course, though some of them are a bit taller." He paused and faced about. "Viking hasn't seen this kind in a long time, so you'd better show it to him first and see how he takes it."

Derf stepped away, and my heart did a funny flipflop, then settled in my boots. I walked my horse forward until his chest almost pressed against the timber. I clucked and held him in place, then clucked again. Viking became instantly alert. I could feel the power of him surge against my legs as I swung him away and came around in a wide circle. I let him break about forty yards back, then asked him to extend his stride as we came galloping in.

What happened next I still can't figure out. My eyes got stuck on the top rail and wouldn't come off. Something inside me quit and telegraphed Viking, for suddenly he lost pace and veered sharply to the right. I left the saddle like a rag doll. The fence exploded in one bright flash with no sound effects. Then I heard Derf say, "Lie still—don't move, Mike."

Derf swam into focus, crouching over me. His hand held the rein, which I followed slowly upward to Viking. A light breeze was lifting his mane. The daylight hurt my head, and I shut my eyes against it. "What happened?" My voice belonged to somebody else.

Derf answered quietly, calmly. "Nothing much, Mike, you just tried to bust up a perfectly good fence with your head." I repeated his words to myself, concentrating on them as hard as I could, then asked him again, "What happened?"

I'm sure I asked Derf, "What happened?" at least twenty-five times before the day was over. Back at the motel, he called a doctor. The doctor examined me carefully. He told me to stay in bed and rest for a couple of days but said there was nothing to worry about—just a plain old concussion, par for the course.

I was caged in that cabin for three whole days. Derf was a good nurse, and even though I fretted and fussed to get going, he insisted that I follow doctor's orders and stay in bed the first two days. Viking was being worked by one of the Green Spring grooms, but I couldn't wait to get on his back again. This overwhelming desire was not motivated by noble intentions. There was a frightening something I suspected about myself, and the sooner I found out the better.

CHAPTER IX

CHRIS CALLED THURSDAY NIGHT. DERF PICKED UP THE phone, then said, "It's for you, Mike."

My brother's voice seemed to come from the next room. "Hello, Mike. How you doing? Why haven't I heard from you?"

"I've been pretty busy, Chris."

A pause. "Mike, I'm coming down to see the race. Bill Uhlar's taking over, and I'll arrive at Union Station in Baltimore at seven tomorrow night. That all right with you?"

I didn't answer, and my brother's voice came over with a slight note of anxiety. "You all right, Mike?"

"Sure, I'm all right. Why shouldn't I be?"

"Okay, Mike, okay. You don't have to bite my head off. Take it easy, boy. See you tomorrow night." Click!

I sat there holding the receiver until Derf took it from my hand and replaced it gently.

On Friday morning I was up at the crack of dawn. Derf was still asleep, and I dressed quietly in the half-light and slipped out the door with my boots under my arm. I got into them while I sat on the front stoop, and then I made a beeline for the stable. More of tomorrow's entries had arrived: two unfamiliar horse vans stood in the parking lot. The gravel crunched too loudly under my feet as I went through it.

Nobody was around, and I made straight for the tack room, then Viking's stall. He had just finished his breakfast. I reluctantly gave him ten minutes to digest it, then tacked up and led him out the back door. I mounted quickly. The sun was breaking through the low overhead as we jogged north to the large meadow and that line fence.

I pulled up thirty yards from it. A dead hush lay over the land, as if the whole world were watching, waiting. My heart was pounding like a triphammer as I tightened the girth and pulled my helmet down a notch, then asked for a canter and began a wide circle in front of the post-and-rail.

Viking knew why he was here. He moved strongly into the bit, with his neck slightly flexed and his powerful hocks driving well under him. As we came around for the fifth or sixth time, I let him stride out and square away into the jump. I clamped my jaws shut and tore my eyes from the top rail, latching them on the woods up ahead. The muffled beat of his hoofs jarred the silence and jerked my eyes down. The fence came at me too swiftly—"Release now!" But my hands snatched back, bringing Viking to his haunches, then straight up on his hind legs and down again so hard I came slithering up around his ears. Sweat stung my eyes, and a thick wad of cotton filled my mouth as I shinnied back down to the saddle. Panic rushed up into my throat, but I swallowed it, fighting for control. "Don't blow up, Mike—for Pete's sake, don't blow up now!"

I knew what was happening. I knew I was driving Viking against the wall of my fear, but I was helpless to stop it. Right now he needed my confidence to go on, but all I could do was freeze and hang back, forcing him to lose his.

I began clashing controls—asking him to move on, then setting him back when he did. The fourth time around, Viking shut off thirty yards back. He'd had it. So had I.

The meadow began to swirl around as though I were seeing it under water. Waves of nausea twisted through my insides, and I slid to the ground and tried to throw up. I retched again and again, but nothing came, only the bitter taste of frustration and defeat. When I tried to remount, Viking wheeled and backed off. His head was up, keeping the rein taut between us. His dark eyes were filled with distrust and suspicion, as if I were his worst enemy.

A groom came up as I led Viking into the stable yard. He took the rein, then peered anxiously into my face. "You feelin' all right?" he asked.

My dry lips stuck to my teeth when I tried for a grin. "Guess my head isn't right yet," I managed to croak. Then I turned away and walked slowly back to the motel.

I slumped down on the stoop and leaned against the doorjamb, my head thrown back, my eyes closed against the morning sun.

Any jump rider, no matter how brave or courageous he may be, can lose his nerve. It may leave him slowly over a period of time or suddenly like a bolt out of the blue. But when it goes, it rarely comes back.

I had heard this many times, but, like the jaywalker, I figured it could never happen to me. During the past year the gray horse had given me a pretty rough time—no doubt about that. I had hit the ground, bounced back, and hit the ground again, and aside from bruised bones and charley-horsed muscles, I'd never given it a second thought. But with each successive jolt a little more heart was knocked out and always a little less returned. Like some malignant tumor it had spread through my body, working from the inside out and gradually gaining control. Now, as I sat with my back to the wall, the future was hopelessly black.

Derf found me an hour later. He crouched down and shook me gently. "Mike, what's the matter, what's happened to you?"

I came forward and stared at the ground, shaking my head. Derf's hand came under my chin and for one second my eyes met his, then dropped away.

"I've got a headache," I lied, then painfully tried to rise.

Derf pressed me back. "Now listen to me, Mike." His voice was soft but steel-lined. "I think maybe you got a harder knock on the head than I figured." He stopped and studied me carefully. "I promised your brother I'd take care of you. I told him that when I thought you'd had enough I'd pull you out, and I think maybe you've had enough right now. I'm scratching Viking for—"

"No!" I crashed in. "No, no! You can't do that!" I lunged to my feet and caught Derf's lapels. "You can't do that, Derf," I repeated. "I started this whole business, and I'm going to finish it—you hear me?" I choked on the words. "Viking is ready, and tomorrow afternoon I'm gonna ride him for the Maryland Hunt Cup if it's the last thing I ever do—" My voice broke, and I sank back down to the steps. How could I tell this man that Mike had chickened out? How could I tell him I had less backbone than a jellyfish and no heart at all? I dropped my head to my knees and sobbed like a kid.

Derf sat down beside me and put his hand on my

shoulder. His voice held a new, gentle note when he spoke. "Easy does it, Mike, easy does it. Viking will run tomorrow, and nobody will ride him but you."

Suddenly I came wide-awake in the small hours of the morning. I didn't know where I was. Then I remembered—this was Saturday, April 30, and at four o'clock this afternoon I would ride Viking for the Maryland Hunt Cup.

Derf was asleep on a cot across the room, and Chris was snoring lightly in the next bed. Our meeting last night at the railway station had been more like a wake than a reunion. Chris had said I looked awful, and he would have said more if Derf hadn't quickly changed the subject. We ate at a nearby restaurant. I barely touched my food, and later Chris followed us out to the motel in a rented car. Everything in Shawan was booked solid, but we got an extra cot and bunked him with us.

Chris told me he was picking up Jenny at the Baltimore airport at one o'clock Saturday afternoon. How could I face her now? How could I tell her that all my brave talk had meant nothing and that she had been right in the first place? A great riding master once said, "Never start anything with a horse you can't finish." And here I was completely committed but incapable of finishing what I had begun.

All the events of the past few days came crowding in and hit me one at a time, then all together. I tried to sort them out, to analyze the basis of this unreasonable terror that was rapidly taking over.

I knew that the size of these fences scared the daylights out of me. At this point I also felt that as a rider I was hopelessly outclassed, that I could do nothing but mess up and disgrace my horse. But worst of all, I had reached the point of no return and my only direction lay straight ahead, regardless of the outcome. The combination of these facts was more than I could handle.

I lay in bed sweating and staring upward until the dark ceiling turned gray with the dawn. I dressed and went outside, then walked aimlessly down Butler Road, away from the stable. The sky paled in the east with the woods coming up black against it. I sat down on a rock and leaned back against a tree, facing the sunrise. The day broke clear with lots of sunshine and blue sky.

At noon Derf and I walked the course. We left the pickup in the general parking area, then crossed Falls Road and tramped diagonally along the fields to the right of Tufton Avenue. Police and state troopers moved about in scattered groups, and there was a handful of early arrivals, even though the race would not begin until four o'clock.

I had a diagram of the course that showed that it ran counterclockwise, twice around, and covered four miles of rolling country. After the twelfth fence you jumped the thirteenth, which stood alongside the third, then the fourteenth alongside the fourth and so on, including the nineteenth alongside the ninth. After that came numbers twenty, twenty-one, twenty-two, and the finish line.

I jammed the map into my shirt pocket as Derf and I approached the starting line. From there the going was slightly uphill with a two-hundred-yard run to the first fence. This structure was built of one-by-six oak boards, double thick on top. There was a hundred-foot spread between flags—plenty of room for any size field to go through.

Derf said nothing as we walked slightly downhill to the second. The most forbidding aspect of this four-footer was the large spreading trees at intervals along its line. Remember to keep your eyes up, I thought. Ride a line, don't diddle, be definite! We continued in silence to Tufton Avenue. A thick tanbark carpet seventy feet wide had been spread over the concrete road. We trudged across it, then bore slightly right and came face to face with the third fence.

There it stood, five rails deep and solid from the ground straight up to four feet nine inches. So this was the baby that stopped Derf and Viking, Mindon Mount, Hubar, Jumping Jack, Black Sweep, and a host of other greats.

Derf was talking, but I was only half listening, for now I was certain that this course called for a horse with a special kind of heart, and a rider with a shockproof brand of nerve. I had the horse all right, but, "Please, God, give me the guts to face these fences."

"Union Memorial," the thirteenth, stood alongside; then

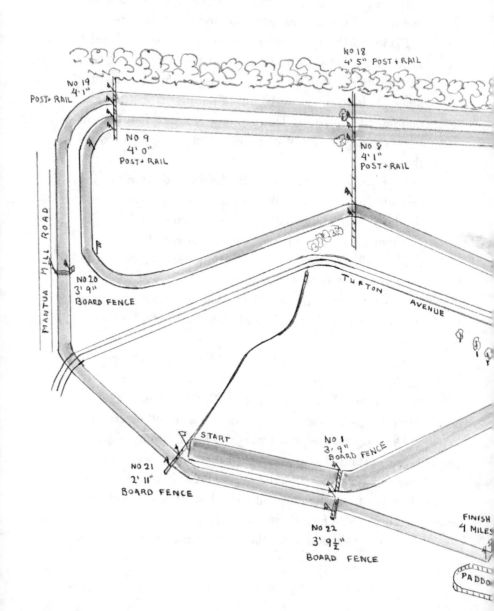

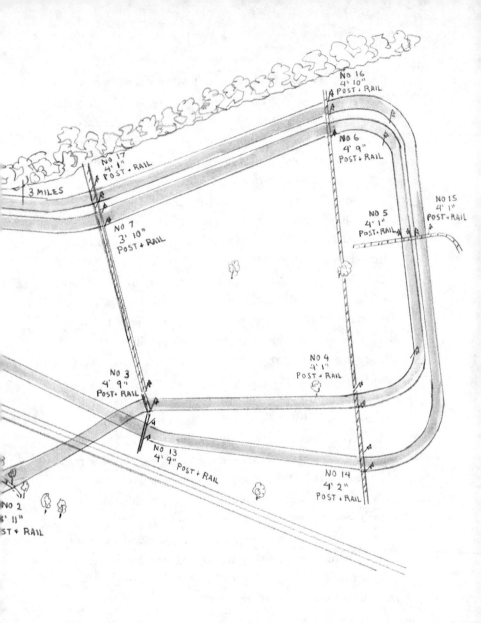

MARYLAND HUNT CUP COURSE
WORTHINGTON VALLEY MARYLAND

came four and fourteen, five and fifteen; and uphill and left to six, which cut down Octavia's Son in '58, and sixteen, which stopped Coup-De-Vite in that same race.

Derf was talking rapidly now. "You jump this pair uphill. They stand four-nine and four-ten, but more like five feet because you come at them from the bottom up. If your horse gets in too close, he'll never get his knees clear, so keep your eyes up and don't ask too late."

We moved on to number seven and the seventeenth, which killed the great Troublemaker in '35; eight and eighteen, each with its own forbidding look, its own challenge—and its own toll of casualties. We crossed Tufton Avenue again, then upgrade over the last two and the two-hundred-yard run to the finish line. We both slumped to the turf. Derf was exhausted—and I was completely demoralized.

It was a little past one-thirty when we reached the parking field. By now the spectators were pouring in. Before the afternoon was over, they would be twenty thousand strong. The car plates said they came from Maryland, New York, New Jersey, Pennsylvania, Virginia, Connecticut. Blankets and picnic lunches were spread out all over the place. There were toy and souvenir venders and ice cream trucks and swarms of children. I could see many more cars parked on the far hillside to the north. All this built around one race that would last maybe nine minutes.

CHAPTER X

I TOOK THE WHEEL, AND DERF COLLAPSED BESIDE ME with a groan. Chris was just pulling up in front of our motel as we drove in. When I saw Jenny get out of his car, I caught my breath. She was beautiful, and for one brief instant I forgot my dilemma. She was wearing a tan trench coat, with the collar turned up against the breeze that ruffled her dark hair. Her eyes sparkled when she saw me. She kissed me, then held me at arm's length.

"You've lost weight, Mike—but you're still very handsome," she added quickly, smiling. "And oh, yes, Marty and Wendy send their very best. Nettie sends you her love."

I felt awkward and self-conscious. Chris called, "Come on, folks. I've got hot coffee and sandwiches. I'm hungry." I couldn't eat, but I downed two cups of coffee—black—then stretched out on the bed.

I must have dozed off, for I was startled awake by Derf's hand on my shoulder. "Time to go, Mike."

I jerked to my elbows, and my heart jumped and stuck in my throat. I could hear Chris and Jenny talking outside. Derf was standing over me, smoking a cigarette. My silks were laid out on the next bed.

I remembered seeing a movie a long time ago. I was chewing on popcorn with my feet propped up on the seat in front, watching a matador getting ready to enter the arena. His clothes were laid out just like mine, his two friends standing by—and here I was, maybe ten years later, going through the same thing, with no popcorn.

I got up and dressed as quickly as my fumbling fingers would allow. Derf stalled in the doorway. His hand reached across, and I came up against his arm. "Mike, we won't get a chance to talk again until after the race." He paused, then went on. "I only want to tell you that I know what you've been going through this past week. But just remember this, there isn't a rider out there today who isn't scared. A man is nuts or a liar if he tells you otherwise." He turned quickly and went down the walk to meet the car.

We dropped Derf at the stable and headed for the paddock. Chris, Jenny, and I were the first to arrive. The hillside above was filling with spectators, but the paddock itself was empty except for a few officials. The blackboard said two horses had been scratched, leaving seven. The purse was $10,000. Gunhill topped the entry list, and two minutes later his rider entered the paddock. I caught Al Mead's eye, but he didn't seem to recognize me; his concentration had begun.

The afternoon was clouding up, and Chris draped a sports coat over my shoulders. Two more jockeys arrived. One was Paul Tagert, Jr., who would be astride the favored Black Watch, winner of the Sand Hills Cup at Stony Brook and the Western Run Plate last week. The other rider was Richard Stainforth, the nation's leading amateur steeplechase rider in 1979.

Suddenly, over the brow of the hill above the paddock, an outrider in a pink coat appeared. He was mounted on a bay horse. He picked his way slowly down the slope, followed by the timber horses and their handlers. I spotted Viking instantly. My heart filled with pride, but an oppressive guilt had a stranglehold on my insides. The sheet that covered his body was deep blue, with gold trim, and his head was high, proud and bold. He moved lightly with a bounce. Derf was leading him, hand locked on the bridle rein, trying to hold him to a walk.

By this time the crowd was massed so tightly around

the paddock entrance that for a moment it seemed as if the horses wouldn't get by. Finally a section of snow fence was taken down and the parade of horses came in and started slowly around the paddock track. The whole scene had reached a crescendo of color and sound.

It was almost race time. The paddock was now filled with stewards, officials, owners, trainers, riders—strangers all—gathered in isolated groups and making me feel like a lost soul in no-man's-land. I could see Jenny on the outside of the paddock, pressed against the fencing. When she caught my eye, she raised her fingers to her lips and blew me a kiss. If only the earth would gape open at my feet—if only I could crawl in and hide!

My brother's face seemed dazed and confused as he handed over my tack and took my coat. I lined up for the weighing out. The scale tipped at 168. I stepped down, then moved like a sleepwalker toward Viking. A strange lethargy seeped through my bones, and I yawned constantly as I shouldered my way through. Chris caught up and mumbled something like "God bless you," then turned and was instantly lost in the crowd. Derf saddled up quickly.

Viking was prancing in place, but his head and eyes were turned away from me, sweeping across the confusion and resting on the green hills to the south. What did he recall of the last time? What kind of day was it then—and what did he remember of the course and the third fence and yesterday morning? Ten minutes to go.

A voice called, "Gentlemen, up." The saddle felt hard and cold and slippery. Derf was checking details—safety girth, irons, throatlatch. As we moved around the paddock once more, I didn't feel a thing, only numbness and resignation. Time had finally run out, and all that remained was the race to be run.

At the paddock gate Derf reached up and gripped my left knee. "Good luck, Mike." Then he stepped back, and I was on my own—with Viking.

I went along automatically. Everything around me was hazy, unreal, but cut through by sharp impressions—the strong, pungent smell of wild onions and sweat, the flash of metal, a cough. At the starting line we were lined up abreast, all seven of us. A green-and-gold banner fluttered above. Viking was on his toes, alert, waiting. One horse broke and was brought around on the outside and into position again. The starter was standing in front, then moved down the line and faced about. He raised his red flag. "All ready, gentlemen?"

I was hardly aware of the flag dropping—only a mighty forward thrust that slammed me back in the saddle, my hands up, and both feet thrust forward. I tried to bend my body into Viking's line of motion, but his rapid acceleration pressed me back. The surging field swept him along with it and carried us over the first and second fences without any help from me. Viking was fighting for his head, trying to move on, but I bounced there like a dummy, frozen at the controls, not giving an inch.

We came barreling into the third fence, but my mind got there first and stopped dead, blacked out—and as Viking's hocks came under and sent him over, my hands jerked back on his mouth, bringing his quarters down on the top rail with a sharp crack that almost dropped him headfirst on the other side. The jar threw me against his neck. I clung desperately like a drowning man, then slid sideways and down, meeting the earth on my feet. I staggered ahead as Viking wheeled to face me, for I still had a death grip on the rein. He plunged backward and brought me to my knees. His eyes were wild, white-rimmed, accusing.

Then suddenly, like a bolt out of the blue, the realization of what I had done to my horse struck me with an impact I will never forget. I had betrayed him! I had given Viking a second chance at the Maryland Hunt Cup, then had taken it away from him again at the third fence.

The earth still vibrated with the echo of pounding hoofs, for only seconds had passed. Viking was braced against the rein I still held. He began backing rapidly away from me as I came up off my knees, but I followed him relentlessly until his quarters rammed against a section of snow fencing that paralleled the track. There was still a chance to catch the field! He arched his neck and snorted with impatience as I quickly slid the rein back over his head. I caught a handful of mane and vaulted up to the saddle as Viking leaped ahead. In two bounds he found

his stride, then leaned forward into the wind. He knew I was with him now. We had joined forces at last, and from here on, win or lose, we were in this race together.

My fall and rise had carried us far to the right side of the track, and we came on from there in a straight line, angling left into number four. The rails rose up and swept under. We cut the red flag on the turn so close it almost came with us; then we squared away and thundered on to the fifth. The field was dropping out of sight over the brow of the hill. "Come on, Viking!" Number five went by, then the red flag and turn left into six. One of the leading horses had chopped out a top rail. We came pounding uphill, jumped the gap right in stride, and rolled on along the woods. Just before the seventh we passed the "woodchopper." His rider was on the ground, frantically trying to remount, but the picture blurred out and fell away through the rushing wind. I lost count of the fences. They came at me too fast—and went by the same way.

Viking was running big now, closer to the ground, and moving ahead with long ground-eating strides that drove the earth rocketing past like the midnight express. Turn, turn, gallop and jump. Another fence shot by, then the halfway pole—then jump again. We were running parallel to Tufton Avenue on our right; "Union Memorial" lay dead ahead. The entire field loomed into focus almost fifty yards up front. I asked for more, and Viking gave it to me—an extra something that came from the inside and sent his neck straight out with his ears flat back and the green turf spinning away.

A splintering crack of timber! Somebody was down on the thirteenth! I checked my horse, trying to see what lay ahead, then let him go and asked too soon. He stood off and reached for the top rail. It was a bad fence, all sprawled out, off-balance, but we made it, then scrambled for thirty yards and recovered and plunged on. I caught a glimpse of a gold silk jockey on the ground.

Three horses were soaring the fourteenth almost together; just beyond, two more were already going into the turn. As they all swung left into fifteen, I could see one of the horses had no one aboard. We were hot on their heels now, breathing down their necks. Viking was beginning to feel the pace, snorting with every stride, but still going strong—upgrade, left, and the sixteenth bold and stark against the sky.

The riderless one quit and wheeled inside, smashing into one horse and blocking another. I didn't hear a sound as a black horse hit hard and turned over. We were riding his tail, fighting for position, and never had a chance to change our line, so we drove right on through and over the top. We touched ground and jumped again, for the downed horse was rolling directly in front—black belly turned up—thrashing steel hooves—and as we flew over I hoped his rider wasn't under him.

We were in the clear now, with only two horses four lengths in front. I didn't know what was happening be-

hind because I never looked back. Seventeen, eighteen. We took the nineteenth together, three abreast, and zoomed into the turn like a cavalry charge. I had the inside track, but the blue-and-white rider went wide and lost ground. We were alongside Gunhill now. A steady stream of white faces whizzed by, a solid board fence came at us—then downgrade and across the tanbark strip, neck and neck, stride for stride, and going home! A horse was coming up fast on my left. The blue-and-white rider had caught up and was making his bid. It was now or never. "Let's go, Viking!"

Twenty-one—all together. And straight ahead up the long slope the last fence was waiting. It came rushing toward me, but I kept my eyes glued on the horizon. Gunhill was a half-length in front, but it seemed as if all three horses jumped as one. The left-side horse struck and faltered and dropped back. Gunhill's jockey was yelling something over and over again, his bat rising and falling.

A swelling roar engulfed us as we came down the middle of the track, a couple of dive-bombers converging on one target, throttle wide open and the earth leaping up to meet us. I was stretched out flat along Viking's neck, my eyes squinting against the cutting wind, my hands reaching, my legs driving—and Gunhill's head was at my knee as we thundered across the line.

I knew we had won. I came up in my stirrup irons, taking the weight off my saddle. We slowed down gradually, coming around in a wide arc. Tension drained rapidly from my body. I could feel Viking's sides pumping under me. His head was way up, swinging right and left, with nostrils blood-red, distended, blowing hard. The rein was lathered white against his neck and slippery in my hand, and I was blowing just as hard as he was.

The cheering crowd poured in and wrapped around us. I could see Derf pushing his way toward us. He grasped Viking's bridle and cleared a trail toward the paddock.

Once inside, I raised my bat to the steward and at his nod slid to the ground. When I touched earth, my knees buckled, but Derf had an iron arm around my shoulders and a mighty grin all over his face. "You did it, Mike! You did it!"

Derf quickly untacked Viking and passed the tack to me for the weighing in. Suddenly I spotted Jenny making her way toward me through the crush of spectators. I stepped forward to meet her and took her in my arms, saddle and all. My knees were still shaking, and I was unable to speak. Chris came up and gripped my arm as if he couldn't let go.

We all pressed toward the winner's circle. When I held the glittering silver trophy in my hands, I thought, This has to be the greatest moment in my life.

That night I slept like the dead and woke in the late morning. Chris had already taken Jenny to the airport. She had left a note for me: "Didn't want to wake you. See you at home." I dressed quickly and stepped outside, breathing deeply the cool spring air blowing gently up Worthington Valley. The nightmare of the last few days and the third fence was in the distant past.

When I opened the door to his stall, Viking swung around to meet me and shoved his muzzle into my outstretched hand. I had been anxious about that hard rap he had taken on the third, but he walked out sound and unmarked, with only his tucked-up flanks to indicate the strain of yesterday's race.

Later, when I was on my knees, wrapping his legs for the trip home, an elderly gentleman with a warm, kindly face walked up to us. He stood there for some time gazing at my horse, but I kept right on about my business. I was making the final tie on the last leg when he spoke to me.

"My name is Jon Whitcomb," he began. "I owned this horse a long time ago." His hand rested gently on Viking's shoulder. "He's a great horse, and he ran a great race yesterday. I'd be proud to have him in my stable once more." He glanced over at Chris, who was standing by, and asked, "Would you consider selling him back to me?"

I came to my feet as Chris quickly stepped to my side and answered for both of us, "Sir, we appreciate your offer, but this horse is not for sale."

We arrived back home decked in glory. Even though some people thought we should go on racing, I saw no point in it. Viking had finished what he had started, and so had I.

GLOSSARY

Ask   Signal horse to jump

Barrel   Section of horse between forequarters and hind-quarters

Barway   Rails across entrance to a field

Bat   Crop or whip

Bit   Part of bridle, usually of steel, which is inserted in horse's mouth and to which reins are attached

Break smoothly   Start smoothly

Bulge   Hindquarters of horse swinging too wide on turn

Canter   Slow, collected gallop

Check   Slow down

Class   Division of competition at a horse show

Come in under   Jump too close to fence—sticky

Coop   Fence shaped like a chicken coop

Dressage horse   Mount trained in advanced "high school"

Fast track   Racetrack with good footing conditions

Field   Assembly of fox hunters

Flank   Area on a horse between the rib cage and hind-quarters

Flat race   Race with no jumps

Footing   Ground conditions

Girth   Strap that goes under horse's belly to keep saddle in place

Ground   Fox goes into his hole.

Hack   Ride at slow, easy pace; no jumping

Hand-gallop   Gait that is faster than the canter but slower than the extended gallop

Height of horse   Horses are always measured from the highest point of the withers to the ground in "hands" of four inches, with the figure following the decimal point representing inches. 16.3 = 67 inches.

Hocks   In this case refers to hind legs of horse

Huntsman   Person who hunts the hounds and is in charge of the kennels

Jump big   Takeoff for fence a good distance away, but safely and with room to spare

Jump in stride   Jump smoothly from a canter or gallop without increasing or decreasing pace

Lead When a horse canters, he leads off with either his left or right leg.

Lunge line Long rein attached to halter

Master Gentleman leader of the hunting field

Millbrook Fence made of rough-cut timber poles placed parallel, one on top of the other, to any given height

Open jumper A horse that is judged on how high he can jump

Outrider Rider who leads racehorses to track

Paddock Small enclosure for horses

Pick up horse Get horse in condition

Pinned To be awarded ribbon at horse show

Pivot Training movement in which the horse keeps his hindquarters in place and moves his front end around it, or vice versa

Point-to-point Cross-country hunt race over obstacles

Pop A warm-up jump

Pulley rein Emergency brake. One hand is braced against horse's neck, the other pulling back on rein, thus giving the rider maximum leverage.

Quarters Rear end of horse

Rate Regulate

Reach Unsafe jump. The horse takes off too far from fence, must then reach out in midair to clear it.

Round A ride over a course of fences

School Practice jumping

Shut off Quit

Snaffle Bit that is jointed in the middle and works with one pair of reins

Snow fencing Light picket fence held together by wire and used as temporary boundary

Soft Refers to a horse with a good mouth, one which will respond to minimum hand pressure.

Stand off Jump fence from safe distance—neither too close nor too far back

Steeplechase Race over fences

Sticky Jump too close to fence

Strong Hard to hold

Tack room Area where saddles, bridles, and other horse equipment are kept

Take back Slow down

Take hold Horse gets the bit in his teeth and can become uncontrollable.

The going The footing conditions

Timber horse One which races over timber fences

Timber-topper Timber horse

Trappy going Ground conditions that are muddy or uncertain

Twitch Tourniquet applied to horse's upper lip to distract his attention; an instrument used to subdue a restless horse

Two-track Traveling in two directions at once, forward and to the side

Weighing in After race jockey goes through same procedure as weighing out.

Weighing out   Before race jockey must be weighed with saddle. Minimum weight allowed is 165 pounds. If he is below this weight, the difference must be made up by carrying lead in special saddle pad.

Well-mounted   Mounted on a good horse

Wither   Ridge of bone between crest of horse's neck and top of his back

About the Author

Sam Savitt has written and illustrated many articles for horse magazines and more than one hundred books for adults and young readers, including *Draw Horses with Sam Savitt* (Viking). Mr. Savitt is the official artist of the U.S. Equestrian Team and produces the well-known Sam Savitt Horse Charts. He and his wife now live on a farm in North Salem, New York, where he continues to paint, write, and ride and school horses.

Sam Savitt was inspired to write *A Horse to Remember* after attending the Maryland Hunt Cup Race—the most grueling of all timber races. He says, "Before the race I walked the course and examined the fences—one at a time. I realized this race called for a bold class horse and a rider with a shockproof brand of nerves. I have ridden and schooled horses for many years, yet it was easy for me to visualize a rider losing his nerve when he saw what this race demanded."